Dressing for Hope

LORNA JACKSON

GOOSE LANE

© Lorna Jackson, 1995.

All rights reserved. No part of this work may be reproduced or used in any form or by any means, electronic or mechanical, including photocopying, recording, or any information storage and retrieval system, without the prior written permission of the publisher. Requests for photocopying of any part of this book should be directed in writing to the Canadian Copyright Licensing Agency.

Published by Goose Lane Editions with the assistance of the Canada Council, 1995.

Cover photograph © Rob Blanchard. Cherub detail from "Venus and Amor als Homigdieb" by Lukas Cranach the Elder.
Book design by Julie Scriver.
Printed in Canada by Tribune Printing.

10 9 8 7 6 5 4 3 2

Canadian Cataloguing in Publication Data

Jackson, Lorna Mary, 1956-
    Dressing for hope
    ISBN 0-86492-167-5

I. Title.

PS8569.A35D74 1995   C813'.54   C95-950243-2
PR9199.3.J33D74 1995

Goose Lane Editions
469 King Street
Fredericton, New Brunswick
CANADA   E3B 1E5

I
Counting Ties

Counting Ties   **11**
Play Dominoes   **23**
Enough Force to Cause Serious Injury   **35**
Introduction to Calculus   **47**

II
Round River

Round River   **61**
Dressing for Hope   **77**
Science Diet   **91**

III
Elite Hotel

Elite Hotel   **109**
Magnetic Creeping   **125**
Grief Work   **135**

for my sisters

I
Counting Ties

Counting Ties

That was my lover on the phone. From his perspective, our situation is big enough and ugly enough to survive a week or five days. It better be because what about the times he will travel overseas with his wife? Over high seas, making high fidelity. Or when he has to move away and I don't want to tag along? Will I expect him to call every day? I'm the one who fell in love with a Manufacturer's Representative, a wife harbourer. We are the sum total of our choices and, oh boy, I better take responsibility for the ones I make and quit complaining.

At seven in the morning, the whole world wakes to the sound our voices try to make under my covers, over the pouring rain. He maintains it has been less than a week, five days by his clock. My right knee aches and pains from the rain and sleepless nights; the thrill of sensation returned shoots head to toe. My lover's voice roams the earth: we should do some re-thinking about "us."

Re-thinking.

In 1968, when I was twelve, my father called from the city newspaper where he worked and said he might be late coming home; he didn't come home that night. There was a province-wide search for my father. Three months of nights went by before he finally turned up. Hair dyed black, folded up identification with an alias typed on: mythomania. His memory was shot. Stress, past or present or anticipated, had pushed him off the deep end, snapped the waistband of his brain, and he had vanished.

But there was no divorce and I worried about that. Back then, every child with a television worried about that. When he came out of Vancouver General Hospital, Mother tended him as if he was a crippled pup or a draft dodger. We had to smooth off the edges of our conversations, answer the phone before too many rings, put the butter back in the fridge. I played cards with him whenever he felt like it. He was still better than me at cards, even with a crummy memory. "Milly, my girl, luck is on my side." He didn't laugh much at first; it came back eventually, just like he did, like his memory did. Mother's edges smoothed off, too, and she was never the same. She and my father became a world, a location where relatives were not welcome but where relative strangers were. She turned to altruism, causes without affect. A crusader, looking so bereaved and so bereft. She ignored family.

Every time I lose a lover or can't find the one I want, it feels the same as those three months when I was twelve, when strangers would call up and report they'd seen my father riding an escalator in some city: Seattle, Victoria, Edmonton. They thought they could see him; I watched the back yard.

On the phone just now, my lover decreed we should re-think our *relationship*, the wisdom of it. Its appropriateness to each other's wants and needs. How effective is this *relationship*. Bottom lines, last lines, dotted lines all strung out . . .

"This feels so familiar," I said to him.

"Oh, don't hold me responsible for what hasn't panned out in your past. I can hardly be blamed for mistakes you've made. You don't think I feel this as much as you do? You don't think I'm sorry this didn't work out? Sometimes you seem to think – and this is very annoying, Milly – you seem to get the idea that you are the only one who feels pain. Or you think your pain is better quality

than mine. Or more significant because you are a woman, a nurturer, a potential breast-feeder. I feel pain, too, lady. I feel like I've been kicked in the balls."
  "Did you say 'licked'?"
  "You heard me. Don't."

It is ten a.m. and I am re-reading stockpiled and shabby newspaper articles about my father's disappearance and reappearance. They quote Mother saying things I cannot imagine issuing from her. They invent a language for her; it is not her voice. Low fidelity. And the picture they chose of my father has him grinning up at something – fighter planes, or hard rain – like a maniac, like a mentally deranged black and white man from a silent movie. I would not have recognized him without that fathercalm written all over his face.

When my father left, we had to put a tracer – the police called it a howler – on the phone, because he called periodically. He'd call to say he'd be a little late for dinner, not to wait for him, carry on without him, just carry on. The police tried to trace the calls, but that never worked. Once, he just moaned over the phone. I answered that one and I dropped the receiver to the floor because I thought something dangerous or dirty was happening. My grandmother called later, said he'd done the same to her so it had to be him.

It is noon at my kitchen table, early Canadian soft fir. I can see and touch where a boyfriend pressed down too hard and left letters etched into the finish. I can almost read whole words. Windows surround this table; hard rain keeps me off the streets.

This is the third time today I have read the letter from my foster child, a small resident of El Salvador. It is a translation from one thin sheet onto another, firm, hard foreign ballpoint pen into manual typewriter haze. He is five, so it is probably a translation of his mother's imagination, a re-write. His name is José Luis Flores.

> *Dear Lady;*
> *I greet you sincerely hoping you are fine*
> *Now we are in winter and it rains a lot but it*
> *will be over soon Thanks to your help I can go on*
> *Rain helps us to get our food corn and beans*
> *We live far away from the capital city and my mother*
> *gets wet when she comes back from work*
> *Since I got your first letter I was very happy*
> *I hope we can keep in touch I pray God bless*
> *and protect you*
> *all the time*
> *until next time God bless you*

Is this the way José's mother articulates feelings or bitches about the weather? "Thanks to your help I can go on." This line slipped between little boy rattle-on about rain and food. He shows me his mother, an authentic detail: she gets wet coming home. But here is the mother speaking: I wonder who sees me trudge, if Canada cares?

This woman is younger than I am. She has three children, a husband, a sister and brother, a mother and two fathers living in her dirt-floored house. Compressed earth walls. Zinc roof. Firewood and gas to cook meals. Every day is a barbecue: rice, beans, tortillas, eggs. Water from a spring. And rainwater. *Usually they do not boil their drinking water. They dispose of garbage by burning it.* They own the house. Catholic. Rosario Flores, Rosie. She is a seamstress, seemstress. *Portrerlillos Community, La Libertad.* $55.97 US per month. Plus my contribution to quality of life, pursuit of happiness. And my transletters, too little too late.

This week, I waited for my lover to call; I waited for the rain to stop. This week rained five days. We are a rain forest. He has called; my lover called re: thinking.

I read José's translation again, taste it, smell it. And then my clippings from when Father vanished/turned up:

> He told his wife that he might have to stay overnight in the Nanaimo Lakes area on Vancouver Island, but that he would phone her if this was necessary. He did not telephone her.

I try to picture Mother handling the press, the pressing for details. She was never capable of straight answers, and I wonder if reporters were as off-put by her evasion as I have been. I am amazed that she does not itemize the plight of the homeless in Vancouver, the recklessness of the Vietnam War, the need for global disarmament and compassion. The Family of Man. Newspapers choose not to print some things. What about the need to neuter our pets, where's that?

> "I am going to Vancouver Island today to look for myself," said Mrs. Jameson.
> Jameson is a man of moderate and regular habits. He's about five foot ten, and left home wearing a brown suit.

Men wearing brown suits; women follow suit, look for themselves on some island. Women look for themselves in men wearing brown suits on some island. Moderate and regular habits.

It is afternoon. I live a block from Royal Columbian Hospital and I go there, running through rain, slipping, to see my grandmother. She is recovering from a series of strokes, though "recover" may not fit someone of her age and attitudes. She is eighty-one and has never been cheerful. Her husband is dead, her only son is dead; one sister wanders away from Extended Care facilities; if she was a hobo, they'd say she counts ties.

The strokes have done some appealing things to my grandmother's mind. We have never liked each other. I have always been too big for my britches; she has always been – she used to pay me fifty cents to keep my thumb out of my mouth for an afternoon. I imagine tiny tsunamis ploughing into dormant brain cells of imagination and spirit.

She is on the eighth floor. Her window overlooks Fraser River commerce, Sapperton railroad tracks, freeway access, Labatt's brewery digital clock, a windshield repair shop. She knows who I am but believes she adores me and that I can swallow some of her fear. We hold hands for the first time. She is tiny on that big hospital bed: "This morning, at seven, the ferry boat came right up to the window and I watched your mother and father get off it. But they never came in. Maybe they've gone home to change. When will they return to the Island? The ferry was overloaded. So many people. I guess the holiday season is upon us. Take a look out that window, Milly. See if the ferry is still docked. The big CPR, the midnight boat. They let you take a drink on that one. And you get your own private cabin. If it's not out there, your mother's gone back already and forgotten to visit. If it's still there, she's changing to come here."

I try to get up to have another look out the window, but she won't let go of my hand. "The rain is really coming down out there, I don't think I could see it if I tried," I say to her.

"Can't you hear it rumble?" She closes her eyes to listen, and is asleep.

I look in her metal table drawer to see if she needs anything, supplies. She is hoarding packets of white sugar, there must be thirty of them; this feels like a drug bust. Her eyes are closed, but she says through variegated lips, "Tomorrow is my one hundredth birthday and they're giving me a party. The man from St. Mary's is coming." She walks the line.

I walk home and am soaked through my raincoat. I have never owned an umbrella; it would be rude in this city, in our beloved rain forest. I check the mailbox for something from my lover though I know the mail came this morning: discount dry cleaning coupon and past-due hydro bill. There's always the chance of special delivery or registered mail. I put the phone back on the hook so he can get through if he's been trying. I make a pot of grandmother tea in Royal Doulton and turn up the CBC. The Mills Brothers plead on behalf of the whole Third World: *Don't fence me in.* And then, on a lighter note, a woman with my name tells me:

> Since the Salvadorean leftist rebels launched their biggest offensive in the decade-old civil war, the world's attention has been focused on the capital of San Salvador.
> Machine guns rattled and mortar fire boomed throughout the area. A helicopter gunship circled overhead firing rockets and strafing the zone with its high speed miniguns.
> 300,000 people, nearly a third of the population of the city, have been cut off from food and water and were pinned down in homes or shelters by the fierce fighting.

I read José's letter again, trying to find some clue as to his safety, survival skills. I wonder if Rosie went to work this morning; I wonder where the money will be if she didn't. And does she say to her children: "Thanks to your help I can go on." Seemstress. The CBC says they hid under their beds. Dirt floors, outdoor latrines. Dodging bullets.

Here, it rains on the dark. I yank the curtains closed and wonder if my body is a provocative silhouette to passers-by. I go back to my own clippings, looking for clues, cover, survival skills. On November 11, 1967,

> Mrs. Jameson says that it is possible that he has suffered a lapse of memory. "He crash landed a plane during the Second World War and suffered a head injury. He still bears the scar, but even though it has never bothered him before it could have some bearing on the case."

These sentences are too long and narrow to be Mother's. She would not say he "bears" a scar and then say it may have "bearing" on the case. There is drama in her prepared statement, and I don't think she would want to emphasize the dramatic. She would protect us from it, from innuendo; downplay.

How would my lover's wife respond to a missing husband? I know her well; we have been friends since grade four. I wonder if she would suspect me immediately. Or would she start with the broken collarbone he got playing rugby, the whiplash he got on the Trans-Canada, the way he behaved when his father died of a heart attack while scarifying the back lawn. My lover has known trauma. Where would his wife start to unravel the mystery of his disappearance?

Six months ago, the three of us rented a Winnebago and sailed to Vancouver Island, the little refrigerator packed with gourmet: rabbit paté, potted meat, pumpernickel, melon and smoked mackerel. Significant old music on the tape deck so we could sing along. I bought a guide to every quaint pub from Jordan River right up to Alert Bay. On the map I marked beaches where we could stop to swim.

My lover drove, I sat beside him. His wife stayed in the house part, in the back, huddled in terror under a grey blanket, holding herself and whimpering in fear. Though the highway was mostly two lanes, she warned him never to pass. When he did, a few times, smooth and careful, she would stand up, teeter, and scream at us, "*You fucking assholes,*" over the slow traffic whisper. When we pulled into the first pub on my agenda, a sunny harmless spot near the southern tip of the Island, she shrieked again: "How could you suggest it? He can't drink and drive. Milly. You stupid bitch. What are you trying to do, *kill us?*" She wedged herself in behind the pedestal table and slumped down onto the bench, moaning while he and I fell in love behind the windshield. We decided to marry each other and have children, happy ones.

Even before sex occurred to us, before it was decided we would have some, I spent money on underwear that only looks good without clothes on. Then he called and said, "The bishop told me they now interpret the 'death' part in 'Till death do us part' as the death of the relationship. I can't leave her yet," he said, "but I want you. Let's at least start something." He sounded promising; is that the same as making promises? Were promises made? "I'll be the one with the rose in my teeth," he said. How would the bishop rationalize this:

> The wife of Vancouver newsman Bud Jameson says she still hasn't given up hope that he is alive. His car was found abandoned in North Vancouver Saturday night and his wallet was found earlier in Burrard Inlet near the Second Narrows Bridge. "I don't know what to do now," said Mrs. Jameson Sunday night after cutting short a search on Vancouver Island when she learned the car had been found. "We'll just have to keep hoping."

My lover's voice this morning: we are re-thinking. I was starting to believe he wouldn't surface at all. I thought about calling his wife but was afraid it would sound suspicious if he never came back and then sent for me. Now he has called. We are the sum total of our choices. This feels so familiar. I want to phone Mother for compassion, but how can I explain this; we have never discussed 1967 or 1968. We do not talk about the search for my father. We discuss increments of liberty and justice; we do not touch on my lovers.

I count ties.

José writes from La Libertad and I see him under his bed. White teeth smile up, manic but lovely. His mother still wet from her walk: "We are in winter, and it rains a lot, but it will be over soon." She consoles me; she prays for God to bless me and protect me all the time. Until next time. There is a howler on my phone; it is me. Tracing myself with my fingertips, my journey from the Island, home and back again in one day. On this table. In all this rain.

Mother rented our basement to a shrubby Vietnam veteran who was here to study physics at university. This was the late seventies. The rooms were nice; she painted everything lemon yellow, used high gloss latex. Shampooed her hooked rugs, found him a good-quality hotplate, and installed a bright light over the basement door so he would have a private entrance. I think a clock radio was provided. Cozy. But in the fall, when all the rain would start and not stop, he woke up in the night – or maybe he stayed asleep for this – and ran out into our back yard, bellowing, tripping and falling to his knees into puddles, his face pointed up to the sky, beseeching whatever was up there to stop it. Our cocker spaniel barked hysterically from my room. My father went downstairs to bring the poor man in; Mother made hot chocolate and cinnamon toast, told me to go back to bed.

I am in my bed, three pillows propped behind me. And finally I get to February 15, 1968:

> Amnesia victim Bud Jameson, 46, Vancouver newsman, thought he had been missing four years when the memory of who he is came back to him in a Nanaimo hotel on Vancouver Island. The manager said Jameson registered at the hotel under the name of Stephens. "He had a whole set of papers in another man's name. He couldn't remember where he got them. He didn't seem to be able to remember news items or politics since 1964."

My lover, I know, is long gone for good. I drop the clippings to the floor beside my bed. I turn out the light and get out of bed. Rain is strafing the zone.

Re-thinking.

All I can do is drop to the floor, slide under my bed, and wait. Wait for the rain to stop and my heart to start and the trees lose leaves snow to fall spring to come and bulbs I never could force them I want them to take their own sweet time.

And José and Rosie can read my letters to each other and he can learn to read Canadian women what happens if some day she doesn't come home from capital city where she works will José search or will it be just as well seemstress threads pulling us all together in the rain and fighting and volleys re think rainforest howler under the bed HELP unreliable information in black and white HELP with no conclusions no wrap rapt HELP ME I howl find him.

Play Dominoes

Everything I own is in this car; I don't own this car. I own a couple of plywood speaker cabinets with sixteen-inch JBLs in them. I own a six-channel amp – three EQ bands out of six work. A beat box. A '63 Telecaster. An Easter cactus my grandfather gave me ten years ago: "Maybe you can make it bloom." A brown check shirt with white pearl buttons. Yellow rope. Three hundred albums and two stacks of back issues, one of *American Artist* and one of *Jugs*. The car belongs to my mother. It's an orange Austin: a loaner.

I left the town of Chase at two this morning. I said I didn't know any country music anymore, said I couldn't fake "Bobby Magee" if my life depended on it. Instead, my last set (last night) started out with Perry Como and finished with Herman's Hermits. I played "There's a Kind of Hush" to the bartender (she clapped) and the owner (he held his head), the only ones left at the end. "Thank you very much. Good night," I said warmly into my microphone. It was the first night of a two-week gig, but I packed my gear to go. The owner approached with flying hands and violent eyebrows, but I said fast, "You don't owe me anything. I had a nice time tonight. Just tell the agent I was too good for the room. He'll understand. He's heard it. And thanks again."

"I don't know why they send me a girl," he said.

It's four in the morning and the car radio hisses like a bad gasket or a leaky rad or a blown thermostat. The steering wheel jerks me around if I go over the speed limit, so I'm just under it. Rigs and cops and me: The Little Lady with the Great Big Voice.

I'm trying to think of a road song to sing to myself, but I don't remember any of the words. It's like I've sucked back all the tunes so they're not songs now. They're breaths; involuntary, quiet, in and out. There's danger in a country song. You read yourself into the turmoil. You're it, a fugitive. *I'm on the run, the highway is my home.*

The back seat's the living room; this shirt's the wallpaper.

When Danny brought his albums and his dirty magazines over for good, moved in with me, he had this shirt with him. Wadded into the bottom of a green garbage bag suitcase. It must have stayed there through his last few moves because when he pulled it out the wrinkles were tiny and firm, permanent like the palm of a hand. In that condition, it looked small enough to be a little boy's favourite; I thought it was a souvenir. *All I have left are a few souvenirs* – that country and western tune he played for me in the bar the night before. But he stood up, clearly a naked man, in the middle of my living room and he tugged at that shirt until it wrapped him up. He smoothed and patted it flat until only the tiniest wrinkles showed. He folded back the cuffs, twice each, made sure they were even on his forearms. A quick look down into the breast pocket (a note? a phone number?).

On a farmer or a square dancer it's gingham, worn in the spring to celebrate winter leaving or in summer to welcome crops, a shroud of plenty. You can work in it, you can dance in it. In my apartment in October, it was a brown checked shirt that came to just below the ass of the man I loved. The way he made sure the bottom button was done up, how his wrists looked thin, the right one brightly birthmarked: something. I leaned back into the couch and raised one knee, knowing my bathrobe would open and convey an invitation. I watched his face for a sign.

He looked up from that bottom pearl button and glanced between my legs, then stared at my mouth without moving his own, blinked quickly several times. He found a spot to focus on between my eyes. "I can still see the stains," he said. Before I could say "What?" he went on. "This is what I was wearing when my father shot himself." We looked at my knee. "I was upstairs with my girlfriend. My mother was below us in the kitchen. I ran down the stairs; my mother and I ran down to the basement. Right then, he pulled it. We'd both felt like something was wrong, but we were too slow, too late." He went to the backs of my eyes; that's where I was hiding out from his story. "Though from my father's perspective," he said, "we probably got there just in time."

That can't be the sun coming up yet. It's not even four-thirty. It must be that fire they were talking about in the bar tonight, last night. I heard every word they said. They think I can't hear because I'm wrapped up in the songs. But I do several things at once. I hear everything.

The smoke coming through the no-draft makes a smell like I have company. Maybe Danny's throwing a party in my living room, and I'm up here in the bathroom trying to stare myself down in the mirror so I'll find the nerve to join them. It's dark out there, in here. Waiting for him to walk in and turn up in the mirror. At this hour, he's not showing. I never should have expected him to do things like that, romantic acts I learned in books; I never should have presumed he could take part. I made him feel he was doing something wrong when he didn't show up. Hindsight, rear view. *Love is a burning thing.* Everyone thinks Johnny Cash wrote that tune. Actually, his wife – June Carter – wrote it; her daughter cut a disco version. I bet the wife wishes she'd kept it for herself; I bet she figures she got burned.

It must have been barely spring because I remember the forsythia annoyed him. My mother had sent me home from a dinner at her house with a car full of leftovers and yellow buds. The long branches filled bottles and jars and pots all through the apartment. Danny said they were too much, they belonged outside in the garden, that the whole thing "wasn't right."

"But we don't have a garden. That's the point of it." I was condescending.

He wouldn't argue past the premise. "Okay, never mind."

The next day, he left on a road trip I wasn't expecting. He loaded his plywood speakers into his turquoise Biscayne and headed out of the city to play music in bars unknown. A life beyond me.

That was the first we'd been apart since the day before that day with the shirt in the living room. I thought I'd die from loneliness and mystery. He called every couple of nights on his breaks; that ensured conversations were no more than fifteen minutes long. This might have been wisdom on his part. I've tried since to maintain romance by long distance; after fifteen minutes questions get hard and short, silences hard and long. Trying to speak a loving touch is impossible; words scratch. After three weeks I had managed to tack those fifteen minute calls into a mile of misunderstanding and was convinced he wouldn't come back.

I wallpapered the bathroom to hold off rigor mortis; I drank red wine to quiet my life. I left the forsythia so long I could smell the rot in the water first thing in the mornings, but I couldn't pour it down the drain.

The calls stopped.

I tried to track him down through booking agents and buddies, but no one knew where he was headed after the third week. I even called one of his old girlfriends, from two hundred miles away, and made her promise he wasn't there. She had the same first name as me – what are the odds of that? But that didn't bring about an alignment. I as much as said she was lying to me and this offended her to tears. A baby cried then, in the background. A man coughed and it wasn't him.

I got tranquillizers from the family doctor; my mother came and slept on my couch. She thought we could share the bed, but that suggestion made my skin crawl. I wouldn't let her touch me after the first hugs of consolation. I muttered things like, "How could he do this after all we've been through together?" I rubbed my arms a lot and stood on alternate feet and curled strands of hair around my index finger.

This melodrama panicked my mother. "What have you been through? What's happened? Tell me," she threatened. It was a mistake to leave her out of things.

I stood at the front window, ran to the side one and back to the front to see if his car was coming from anywhere to stop this. "Nothing. It's just been hard sometimes," I covered up.

My mother probably jumped to the conclusion that we'd had an abortion. What other catastrophe is remembered with such passion by someone my age, what other possibility haunts mothers with such gothic intensity? She was partly right – we had been through that – but it wasn't my turmoil that made it a keepsake, it was Danny's.

Danny picked me up from the clinic at about two in the afternoon. We were home by quarter past two. By three his temperature was over a hundred and his throat was swollen up inside; he couldn't speak, his eyes were small and red. He lay down on the bed, holding his head on both sides, looking like wounded wildlife. From where I was in the living room, I could hear whimpers.

I fell asleep on the couch – an invalid – listening to the voices of Merle Haggard and George Jones comfort me in the key of soft E. When I woke up, Danny was standing above the couch, whispering my name and sobbing and clutching his hair. I thought, "Ah, so this is 'Ramblin' Fever.'" – the song I'd fallen asleep to.

I got him into my arms fast and made him tell me. He'd dreamed he was with his father, fishing on Lake Superior, and they landed a huge mosaic trout. It was alive, moving around. It flickered colours, he said, against the bottom and sides of the boat and onto the face and neck of his father. But the fish scale tiles burned through the aluminum, melted a hole in the bottom and the fish got away. His father was sucked out, too, feet first, right through the hole like he was on an airplane. He was sucked into the big lake; his head was the last to go. Danny grabbed an oar and was saved.

I didn't tell my mother this story; I spared her the abortion intrigue and ran between the windows again.

I saw his car park around the corner; I watched him walk slowly, with his head pointed at the sidewalk, not in any hurry. My mother left immediately, with discretion, out the back way; I wonder if she felt used, left out. I ran down to the first floor landing and collapsed on the top step. I waited for him to come through the door, my fingertips covering my mouth. I looked pathetic.

"What are you doing? What's going on now?" he said, and he was obviously surprised to see me there, and disgusted, too.

"I . . . I thought you weren't coming back."

"Fuck. Quit that. Quit acting. I got fired a couple of times, so? Quit giving me ideas." He walked right on past me, the end of his guitar case bumped my shoulder as he turned the corner up to the apartment. "How much wine have you had?" he called back.

I stayed on the step; I couldn't get up. I don't remember if this was for effect or for real, it could've been either in those days. I wanted Danny to pay attention. I wanted to be in the songs.

He was sitting on the couch still holding his guitar case when I went back up. "It stinks in here," he said.

"Sorry."

"I've found a place to live across the bridge. I'm going tomorrow. I can't handle this any more."

Here's an automotive tip for girl singers on the road. As soon as you know the bar's not going to fire you, when you're pretty sure they'll keep you for the week, ask a waitress, "Who works on your car?" Chances are she'll point to some guy drinking there. Then it's easy. They love it when you sit with them on your breaks, helpless. They love to buy you drinks and wait for you to lighten up. If you're driving a British car, it's better if you can omit that detail when you talk to some of these guys. Some mechanics – especially the small town ones – consider an Austin to be more demeaning than a cold sore in summer. The symptoms are more unpleasant, more costly, and generally less treatable. (If the guy turns out to be the waitress's boyfriend, watch it. She'll get you fired.) My mother has no idea how much maintenance I've managed to charm out of my free time. She just talks about how her car doesn't start, how it doesn't run the same, and she sighs about all the extra miles on it.

"British cars are simply not made for our climate." Even in the middle of the night this car smells like an Austin. Even after a thousand miles I can smell my mother's perfume.

Everything I own is in this car; I don't own this car.

Danny's folks are, or were – well, his mother is from the Ukraine. He complained a lot about how hard it was, growing up in Ontario with parents who could barely speak. He was trying to move ahead and their tongue held him, lashed him. He figured I couldn't grasp this. But how easy was it for me to communicate with a woman who wouldn't put her accent away, who refused to say "bra," who could only bring herself to say "brassiere"? My mother didn't like short-cuts. She said "math" like it made her an outlaw. A woman whose dresser drawer smelled like old rubber and Chanel. Try communicating with that sometime.

Not with my mother; my mother is dead. Only just, so it slips my mind. She did some trick with a rowboat in a bay somewhere on the Island – who knows how she thought it up. She tied herself in and tipped it. She must have been determined because there's that pile of extra rope in the trunk; I noticed it when I put my speakers in tonight, last night. She must have wanted to make sure she had enough and brought extra, just in case it didn't work. She planned everything; she didn't like surprises. I don't get it. I know she was never comfortable with the passing of time.

I need gas. I need my oil checked before I go on; will there be a mechanic here at this hour? I'd do it myself but I don't want to get out. Is it possible to be an agoraphobic from a moving car? *Hello walls.*

I started to play a few months after he'd moved out. Danny used to check the bar after my first night to see if my gear was still set up, to see if I'd been fired. Made me crazy then; I like it now.

Our paths crossed, since we played the same places. Sometimes he'd turn up at my gig at the end of the night, smelling like scotch and looking like an idiot; he always did after scotch. Some guys get real masculine on that stuff; it makes their eyes shine, and their movements get careful and sexy. In Danny, it softened all the starch: in his brain, in his knees. His hands wouldn't stay on straight, his feet bumped into each other. He couldn't laugh, but he wanted to all the time so his mouth stayed wide open. One scotch could do this.

He showed up like that at the Flamingo Hotel one midnight, just as I was packing up my guitar. "Let's get chips and pop and play Monopoly at your place," he said.

"Ya." I used to get the same feeling after waiting through weeks of my mother saying, "We'll see," and finally getting a "Yes, you may."

I had the Austin that night. I followed him across the bridge, a safe distance behind his wide tail lights. I was excited, aroused. It felt significant to be driving my own (I don't own this) car. I was following him, but I was in control.

I've calculated since – so I know. My car stopped – completely – within three feet of the middle of the bridge. There were no warning sputters, it just died there. I watched Danny's tail lights strand me and thought about getting out and running; I saw my mother say "No"; I managed to put on my flashers. Watching cars in my rear view mirror zero in and switch lanes at the last second. Where was he? I turned the radio off so I could hear it all happening, so I could think fast and see straight. Where the hell was he?

It took about a minute for the bridge man – the highway patrol, I guess – to rescue me. He pushed me to the other side. He wanted to know if I'd run out of gas, or some offense he could ticket.

"Nope," I said, "it just stopped," but I don't think he believed me.

Danny was waiting on the other side and he didn't even ask if I was all right. He didn't look silly any more, he didn't look concerned. "What did you do?" he yelled from behind the wheel.

"I was gonna jump," I said, "But that guy said I couldn't leave the car there."

"I'll take you home, but I'm not staying."

His car smelled of mildew and bar smoke and spilled beer. He just dropped me in front of the apartment. No kiss, no nothing. I thought my knees would explode as I opened the door.

"I hope it's nothing serious," he said.

"What?"

"I hope repairs aren't an arm and a leg."

Our last conversation. A week later, one of his buddies brought Danny's stuff over and piled it into my bedroom closet. "I thought I'd do some work on the Biscayne and then bring it over. It's a classic. He would want you to drive it." His hand rested in the middle of my back.

"I don't want it, you keep it. It smells funny."

Alberta. Two more provinces after this and I'm there. I have met Danny's mother once before. We flew to visit her just after the abortion, and I got food poisoning. I still suspect it was deliberate; I was the only one who suffered. But that was a long time ago.

The guy who checked my oil this morning said, "See you on your way back now," and there was something in the way he said it that made my mind up. Money's tight, but once I get rid of Danny's stuff, gas will go farther and coming back won't cost so much.

I looked everywhere in that music for him; I got lost in there myself, followed him into the woods and forgot to leave signs so I could get out. But the country music's bouncing all around this little car. The windows are open and the music's getting sucked out in big gulps of air.

So this is ramblin' fever.

I sing and cackle and make up words. I drive too fast. I own the road.

Enough Force to Cause Serious Injury

Our honeymoon is rank and file tourism, a globe trot back to Becky's favourite hotel. Her warmest spot on the map, she has said; they treated her like royalty there, respected her work, paid up. I gave her the freedom to choose; she picked that hotel in Nakusp.

During boom time, when the bars were topped up and the music was see-through, she used to be Bambi, one of the highest-paid exotic dancers around. One of the best three. Last week, when my parents were over for dinner and a little judgement-passing, the night they contributed the fifty dollars to the honeymoon, Becky recalled those plum times in terms of hardships: "The Ping-Pong balls had been done to death, and the cops were cracking down – sorry honey, but they were. You were just doing your job." My parents looked at me like I was wearing a Marshall Dillon star on my chest. Awed and honoured, they had no idea I was capable of such blatant morality. "So we really had to rack our brains to come up with props that were both tasteful *and* erotic. Every fruit and vegetable in the book. Sheesh."

Becky sat at the head of the table, between my parents – a Rockwell tryptich gone wrong. Mother was eager to please, committed to an interest in Becky's work – a dog on its back. "Emerson, she sets a lovely table," she whispered to me. My dad was committed to cutting roast lamb into bite-sized portions and placing a tiny square of bright mint jelly onto each piece; his arousal complicated the basics. Gravity let go, we all hovered above the new linen tablecloth. My dad said, "Are you quite sure that four-cylinder will make it up some of those grades, Sonny?"

In response to my dad's question, and trying to bring us all back to earth, I said, "I have no way of knowing the answer to that just yet, Dad."

"You bet we'll make it," Becky chipped in.

> DEAR ME: Dinner was bad. Not the food. They treated me like I was from some disadvantaged country or something. Emerson's father kept looking at me eat. He tied his napkin around his neck instead of just tucking it into his shirt. The mother didn't know where to look. She wore a little white lacy apron at the table. She must keep it in her purse. Her hands were under it when she wasn't picking at the lamb (GOOD). They didn't want to hold the baby. Gave us some money for the honeymoon. That was nice. They left early. I can't wait to get going.

With my wife driving, and the babygirl in back, we look like society's essential young family, just starting out. Mid-week, middle of January, maybe a New Year's resolution pledged. "Let's make more time for us while we still can, starting now."

The baby is strapped in and wobbly, weighing scenery, mesmerized by speed, the blur. We parents spell each other at the wheel with personal style. The mom's hair is in one thick, black braid, her body floats inside a huge man's sweater, the sleeves hiked over her forearms, the neck loose, revealing collarbone and throat. Mom hangs on at eight and four, slows, accelerates too harshly into curves, notices signs after the fact, goes too fast to cover neglect. She is an Inexperienced Highway Driver and forgiven.

Just checking, I look back at the babygirl. Eye contact is made and broken at the whim of the child. Her eyes rush back to the great outdoors, shift from drooping, sullen hemlock treetops up to catch a crow fly: black on blue. She sees all. There is the shadow of wisdom in the angle of one eyebrow. Another man's peekaboo. Transparent eyeball.

"I wish this was a convertible in summer," I say. "For the baby's sake."

But this is January in a ten-year-old Datsun hatchback. If the baby was any taller, maybe if she was a boy, there'd be a headroom problem. The car seat suspends her in mid-air; fat legs dangle and pump. It is January and road crews work stubbornly to keep the Trans-Canada Highway safe for us. It is the honeymoon. It is sooner than it looks.

The car has been competent. For the steep parts, we hold our breath and lean forward. The speed hits bottom, and we want to shift to a gear lower than first. It all slows down to a reluctant next to nothing. The babygirl looks alarmed by the pace, whimpers for the blur, pouts and kicks. Becky chants brightly, "I think I can, I think I can," but doesn't know where her makeshift mantra comes from. She thinks it is affirmation and visualization and wants me to hook up to the power. But I can remember the original; the first version is always the best. I see a silvertone cowcatcher grin. Or was it a tug-boat chugging through whitecaps and deadheads?

We hit a stretch of hard-packed snow; trucks have made it bumpy and uneven. The car is still equipped with the original Macpherson struts; they are impossible to fix at this late date.

CAUTION : The coil springs are under considerable tension, and can exert enough force to cause serious injury. Disassemble the struts only if the proper tools are available and use extreme caution. Special Tool ST3565s001 or variations of that number.

Though bound and determined by a serviceable nursing bra, Becky's breasts bounce. *(In this type of suspension, each strut combines the function of coil spring and shock absorber.)* "Yipes," she squeals, and takes one hand off the wheel, brings it to a breast and lovingly lifts, cups her whole palm around it; she moves it gently clockwise.

"Let me get that for you." I reach past the stick shift.

"Don't. I'm leaking. It's nicer if I do it myself."

I touch the back of her hand, put my hand over hers, over the breast, feel a kuckle where a baby-ravaged nipple could be. "Want me to drive?"

"Nah."

"Want to stop for a while?"

"No way. Wait till she cries. Read to me."

"Your choice." I flourish. "Either *Chilton's Repair and Tune-Up Guide* – you've already heard the sexy parts. Or more of Van Gogh's letters."

She moves her hand to cover the other breast. That one is slightly larger, firmer. "Read the letters," she says. "Flip to the end and read from the last ones."

I find the letter from May, 1890, and read to her in a voice shaken by rough terrain:

> And things may yet get better, I still think that it is mostly a malady of the South that I have caught, and that the return here will be enough to dissipate the whole thing. Often, very often, I think of your little one and then I start wishing he was big enough to come to

the country. For it is the best system to bring them up there.

There is sudden fresh snow and rich quiet, a pocket of bliss. The trees are full of it, the highway turns smooth and soft. "Ahhh," she sighs and puts both hands on the wheel. "Finish that one and then stop." Summers with my mother and dad, driving to Okanagan sun in a long blue Parisienne: "Put the book away, Emerson. Reading in the car will only ruin your eyes and make you want to throw up." I choose a letter from July; she won't notice it's a different one.

> I hope with all my heart that the intended journey will give you a little distraction.
> I often think of the little one. I think it is certainly better to bring up children than to give all your nervous energy to making pictures, but there is nothing for it, I am — at least I feel — too old to go back on my steps or to desire anything different. That desire has left me, though the mental suffering from it remains
> Handshakes in thought,
>
> Yours,
> Vincent

"That's enough," sighs Becky.
"Wait," I say, "The last one's good. Listen."

> ... you have your part in the actual production of some canvases, which even in the cataclysm retain their quietude.
> For this is what we have got to, and this is all or at

least the chief thing that I can have to tell you at a moment of comparative crisis. At a moment when things are very strained between dealers in pictures by dead artists, and living artists.

"Did he sign it with the handshake thing?" asks Becky.
"It's not signed."

She gives the okay for some music, and I slide Vivaldi in; London Philharmonic, Albert Hall. My forehead rests against the window, I watch lumps of snow tumble through the trees, the branches rebound and twitch. The baby sleeps. Becky tries to sing the words from an Everly Brothers song – it sounds like "Kathy's Clown" – to fit into the Vivaldi. She swears they are the same song. Extra notes, stray syllables crunch.

DEAR ME: I don't know what's wrong. Maybe it's because my tits are always so sore, but I just don't want him touching me. And I feel bad because he wants to. I used to love it in the car. What's going on with me?

I know it bugs him when I drive, so I get him to read to me. It calms him down. I'm used to driving alone. I put 20,000 miles on that car, and now he wants to teach me to drive. He's teaching me about music and art, though. Sweet. I wish he'd do more with the baby. I wonder if it bothers him. I wonder if I'll have any babies with him.

The whole town remembers her. We are stopped on the street by small parades of mill workers who slap sawdust from their jeans, move their hats back, lift their steel toes high to salute beauty. Black dogs bark from flatbeds. The community newspaper wants to do a story about her – before and after: "Duchess Weds Commoner."

The owner of the hotel stocked our room with peach cider and a fruit basket and I hunt for connotations. It is our first night and the hotel provided an off-duty waitress to babysit so we can celebrate Becky's return with an evening downstairs.

Most of the bar is like a laminated log cabin, deer heads and horns stranded high up, filthy. High gloss varnish on the tables. On the walls, ancient dollar bills trapped. The pool room is prefab and conspicuously attached: a tragic Gyproc flaw joins two worlds. No neon. The felt, though, is brand new bright green.

The music is played on trash can lids. There is little primitive bass drum thump, but a young woman strips, does her best to hold the attention of the men in the room using only a thin sound system. Dominic, the owner, explains confidentially that the men enjoyed her act for the first couple of nights, then the novelty of her skin colour wore off. They had seen a black woman naked now; no more surprises. And since she brought her white boyfriend, she won't be asked back.

"She could use a good PA with some bottom end," I suggest.

"Wouldn't help. It's not the sound in a town like this."

I could have predicted the woman on the little stage would catch my eye during her performance and try to hold it, especially when she is down on the patched carpet, completely exposed and scissoring. They always pick me out and I never know where to look. I am always a man in uniform. I try to look pleasant and noncommittal. I try to take part in her show in a passive way, but Becky is measuring my participation. "I think she has potential," I say, in response to Becky's "Well?" I wonder if the boyfriend is here.

"Too much meat, too many muscles. Nice legs, though. Pretty

smile and all that," says Becky. I slide a hand down the back of Becky's hair, grab a handful and tug gently.

Wrapped in white fake satin, the woman strolls over to the bar and asks for a glass of water. Her skin glistens. The bartender takes more time than is necessary and makes his point. He treats her like she is a troublemaker, an undesirable.

A rock band fills in the blanks on the stage and I dance with Becky to a Rolling Stones medley that goes on forever. It is done deliberately; they're adding any song they know to keep her dancing, accumulating tempo. She is the expert and all eyes are on her; the pool games stand at attention. In a dress that reveals only long legs and skips everything else, she is an enigma. I have never been much of a dancer. I nod to the guitar player; he nods back and then raises his eyebrows at the bass player. The music falls down and stops. The pool games at the back of the room start up again; I tumble into my chair and swallow a lot of beer. Becky kisses me on the neck and leaves to feed the babygirl. But she loiters at tables, puts her hands on the hard shoulders and backs of strangers.

The black stripper watches, turning a second glass of water between her breasts.

> DEAR ME: He watches his feet when we dance. Oh well. It's so nice to be back with people who don't judge me. They like me for what I am, not what they want me to be or what they think I am. I'm drinking too much but it doesn't seem to bother the baby. I'M ON HOLIDAYS!
>
> There's a black chick with no props. She picked Emerson out, of course. I don't think she meant anything, but I got jealous anyway. I don't like it when he looks at other women, especially when I'm drinking

and I get so emotional anyway. I wish I was more mature for him. The paper wants to interview me. Ha! Well, back to the bar. I'm going to feel rotten tomorrow.

"What keeps bread on your table, Emerson? How does a guy go about keeping Bambi in pantyhose?" Dominic asks the first question of the evening. It has been statement of fact, wit, innuendo and plenty of long pauses until now.

"I'm with the Vancouver Police Department. That's about all I can tell you."

"I hear you. Don't go any further. Happy to have you in Nakusp. And I'm glad for Bambi. She deserves a man like you. We're all glad she's safe." Safe from what, and how do I go about protecting her from it?

There is a feeling in my arms and hands that Dominic may be the father of the babygirl. He is, after all, the owner. In a split second, I see myself alone, at the wheel, coasting back down steep grades in neutral, chanting, "I think I can, I think I can." Telling my mother and dad the story. Maybe I'll just write them. There is a resemblance.

"I gotta get home. The wife's gonna think I'm up to something." Dominic dumps almost a full glass of beer down his throat and waves goodnight to the whole bar.

The sex we have is laced with moping and jumped conclusions. I accidentally bring the black woman into bed, looking at the landscape through her legs. I leave Becky stranded.

It is different with the baby right there. Another man's spy. At dawn, I am still awake. The room smells of out-of-season fruit, Becky's bath salts, Becky. The babygirl's diapers, milk.

Out the window, one of the Arrow Lakes glares back. How deep is the snow on top of it and what makes it glow green like that? Some high school chemical, some fluke of nature that fascinates me but not so I remember details. Like the name of those swimming monkeys, the ones that look like old men at a hot springs.

The baby is alert and anxious to see it all. I lean into the crib and pick her up, shove us both through the curtains and up to the window. One hand behind my back, I close the curtains around us so Becky won't see the light and wonder why I'm torturing her.

The baby's eyes fight to adjust to green sparkle. They close, open, close again, open gradually. Two tiny sneezes. One small fist rests against my face, roots around in my beard and yanks hard, gurgling meanings. I yelp and laugh in monosyllable communication.

"I'll feed her." A cliché, now, from my new wife.

I emerge with the babygirl from behind the curtain and join Becky in the dark, in bed. The same breasts from last night, but this morning they remind me of my mother. Shame, a brief slant of light on my cheek, provokes me to leave them alone. I get dressed and wait to be asked back, re-admitted into the essential young family.

"I'm going for a walk." I am already at the door.

"Take her, too, okay? I need the sleep. I need peace." The babygirl is wide awake, sitting tentatively upright on the bed and looking at me; fists fly. Her top half weaves like a grizzly unsure whether to attack or to go down on all fours and make a getaway. I pick her up, get her into the right clothes for this weather, this hour, and cinch her into the backpack, singlehanded.

"I'm locking the door, I've got the key. Don't open it for anyone." She is under the pillow, one arm around it, holding it tight against her ear.

Enough Force to Cause Serious Injury 45

DEAR ME: I feel awful. Too much everything. It's like he wants to be my father. Must be why he's a cop. Authority stuff. Is that what I need? Someone to fix the car and lock my doors? I thought I was past all that. I don't think every woman who marries an older man is looking for a father figure. I wanted someone who didn't want me just because of my tits. I'm tired of men not looking at my face. He seems so conservative. Even with sex, now. Why didn't I see this before? He never talks about the baby's father so maybe I should bring it up and see what happens. What have I done? Maybe we should've waited.

But there is wind off the lake, along the useless railway tracks through winter trees; it's too cold to have a baby out. It's January. It is Sunday morning in Nakusp and nothing's open. Except there is a blue ice rink and two cars parked at opposite ends of the building; someone's in there.

A boy skates around the ice. It takes him forever to do one lap; his legs are short, his strides hampered by huge pads and weak ankles. His skates are white, handed down from an older sister. Determined.

A woman's laugh somewhere in the seats: it echoes and urges. (Men need to see the face of a woman who laughs like that.) They have seats on the blue line, she and Dominic. She is the waitress who stayed with the baby last night. They are under a Hudson's Bay blanket; no hands are showing. The blanket is pulled up around their chins, stripes go across their necks. Her long black hair hangs down her chest; his toque is pulled over his ears to where his beard starts. Even when the little boy skates in front, they are looking straight ahead, across the ice, down the line.

The little forward watches his feet; there is a temptation to warn about the danger in keeping his head down like that, but I resist. Maybe the boy is just agonizing over the skates, seeing them black and new, his ankles firm and straight. He whispers as he passes.

It is no warmer in here than it was outside. Dominic and his waitress have grown silent; they concentrate with sloppy intensity. The boy's head is still down; he's heading for the goal. His big padded hand rights a teetering helmet. Stick above his shoulders, he races as fast as he can and slams himself into the corners, the stick rattles high on Plexiglas. He has cross-checked himself into the boards. "Oof," he says, and sidesteps until he is in behind the goal. He veers around and screams into white air at the opposition: "IT'S A LONG SEASON ASSHOLE!" Off he goes again, weary from the violence, an old injury giving him some problems.

"You be careful, sweetie," sings the waitress. The boy must hate her for that.

He longs to clear the bench.

Introduction to Calculus

She looked it up. She talked to Murray, the Chinese man at the end of the lane. Herds of Roosevelt elk claimed this part of the island once, rummaged in the salal and Oregon grape, happy to rut. Over-hunted. Twenty years ago, just north of Audra's cabin, hikers found carcasses rotting near the Reserve, the horns and testicles rudely salvaged for somebody's myth. As for the few cows, all that was changed were the large rifle holes through and around their ears. One cow had expelled a luminous, whitish calf. A family plot under cover of wood. The eyes of the elk gone to feed turkey vultures and red-tailed hawks, the lovely skulls just starting to resemble masks.

Barnett left at seven-thirty this morning with their little girl, Mandy. At nine-thirty, Chase phoned to report they had not arrived. "What probably happened was, they took the road through the reservoir but the Water Board keeps the gate locked until nine. So then they doubled back to the highway and they're on their way here right now. I told Barny about that gate on the phone last night but he wasn't listening, I knew he'd do it his way. Fear not, Audone. Call you when they get here." Little Faye in the background cheeping, "Where'Dee? Where'Dee?"

Anxiety takes her like Colombian caffeine. She would turn on the radio, but what's in there are songs from the seventies glorifying the elements: rain, sunshine, wind, fire. There are other ways to go.

He named Audra "Joe" and had her serve him. As in, "Hey, Joe," (chime of fork stirring maple syrup into black coffee) "what is it you do with your life? Outside of bringing me hard eggs, I mean."

"I right," Audra hollers from the kitchen, and she will not look back.

"You write what? Don't tell me you write poems about waitresses and their two-timing boyfriends. Oh, gawd – don't tell me that, Joe." Barnett strikes his own head and face with the heel, flat and back of his hand. "You're not writing about truck stops, are you?" Loggers twitch downcounter. Audra watches that deep, deep space between fork and knife the plate enters; air vibrates from Barnett's grin. She'd like to have a better look, see what his eyes do.

"Hey," Audra shoots and points to Barnett's eyes, "they don't call it two-timing any more. Where've *you* been?" Audra is on a short leash. Pot after bloated pot, rings of discount grind on three Bun-O-Matic elements. Audra and the smell and hiss of wet terry-cloth on hot metal. "Stainless" is just a way to put it.

Raymond from Ray's Hardware says he asked for eggs he could pour and did not get what he ordered. Furthermore, there is lipstick on his juice glass and the toast has been sitting under lights: "It's hard, miss, and it's cold." As if he doesn't know her name by now. There is a phone call from Audra's sister, Dale, and the line cook has the sizzle up so high she can't hear the point at the other end. It's an extortion. She thinks. Dale wants money. She's willing to whimper and steal Audra's soft-boiled heart to get it. "Come by after the rush," Audra shouts at her sister, "take my tips."

"So. What is it you write, Joe? Don't tell me romance."

Audra's left hand starts at the ankle, slides up one cellophane leg and lingers to smooth a non-existent wrinkle below her knee. She stands up to Barnett, hands all over the counter, territorial. "I'm a righter," she says. "All I do, day in day out, dawn to dusk, week after week for three years going on thirty is right what's wrong. Get it? Now tell me I'm smart, leave me a huge tip, and get out, I need your seat." Two steps forward, one step back. "Oh. And listen. Don't you underestimate the role of romance in history."

In bed, she told Barnett about seeing the elk. He said, "Don't tell anyone or ten-to-one some plaid shirt will be out here shooting at whatever snaps a twig. Don't tell Chase, whatever you do."

Audra walked the lane in dusk, watching for a pair of barred owls whose zone is the top of a winded and hollowing maple, searching the windfall for owl pellets tight with vole bones and fur. She'd only heard their hoots in deeper evening. As Audra turned and bent to peer into the golden, cumulous branches, she spotted, in a narrow and spotlit draw across the lane, a bull elk.

"Who'd call that prey?" she thought.

Grey squirrels leapt treetops, crossed the lane with derring-do. The elk whispered off into jungly, five-foot bracken, summer aspen, the fungus of immortality. The fine smell of cedar smoke on wind.

"Are you sure it was an elk? Maybe look it up," Barnett scoffed and bent his shoulders into sleep.

"And who died who might come back as that?" Audra wondered.

No word. Barnett and Mandy off-road, the car seat on the passenger side of the white Ford 4X4. The trip should have taken one hour, though backroads and wrong turns could stretch that estimate. Audra has already jumped to conclusions and circles back to jump again. Barnett always knows what he's doing, and discussion about this "little adventure," as he put it, didn't make it to sensible concerns. "Don't let her see you worry, Joe," Barnett pleaded, his mouth at Audra's ear. He calls their three-year-old "her."

The first morning he was a new face at the counter, Audra pegged Barnett as a man on the rebound – too mouthy, too hungry – and waited for him to get hold of his hindsight. She figured, "Wait till his garden's up and the first hay's ready to come down."

So Barnett dated Audra's sister, Dale. Dale was always available for outdoor nudity and conversations about spiritual wealth versus the other, and Barnett went for all that. Dale smoked Camels and drank scotch. So did Audra, but Dale was thin and long, an outlaw.

When Dale answered the call of an old boyfriend, Barnett had already made Audra's aquaintance and, crops up and hay down, he chased her with the unpredictability of a rebound. In the few years since, whenever Dale turns up for a good mooch, Audra wrestles her own brain: they do it when you're at work, they do it while you sleep, they do it in Mandy's room, they want to do it with you . . .

The marmalade cat appears at the sliding door, her mouth stuffed full of ruby-crowned kinglet, her tail high and big with the hunt.

Bird-lids blink. Fir cones and fallen lichen litter the deck. Barnett's gumboots. Mandy's bug jar. The cat begs Audra to open up, and the tiny olive of a bird drops to the deck, flutters, tries to make a run for it, only to arouse the cat's desire.

 Chase calls to check in. "Don't let your imagination get carried away, Aud-one."

Every so often, Barnett seizes little Mandy's fat thighs with the force of a grown man, turns red in the face and hollers, "You stop kicking me now." And when she kicks more, this time with a plan, Barnett squeezes until her look is transformed. Audra suspects a cycle of some kind but she can't pin it down or keep track: the time Barnett grabbed Mandy's ear to make her stop screaming "NAO NAO NAO" at him; he did the same thing to make her spit out dirt; he smacked her hand for hitting the cat, and her face for biting his cheek. Not much to witness. Audra considers the relationship between smoke and fire; smoke can stay smoke.

 She hauls herself away from the kitchen counter and roams the hall, into Mandy's yellow room. Kidney ache when she gets this tense. A languishing wasp flings itself against Mandy's window screen. "Maybe we should let it go," Mandy would say, her voice rising high in mother-mimick.

 "But that sounds like a dog's name," Barnett had said. His choice had been "Joe."

 "Exactly. I had a beagle named Mandy when I was sixteen and then Barry Manilow did that song 'Mandy' and every time it came on the radio I pictured him dancing with my dog. Their noses, Mandy's hind legs. You don't get it. That name has been on my mind since I was sixteen. It's driving me crazy."

 "I don't know if those are altogether good reasons to name the child 'Mandy,' Joe," Barnett said.

Last night, Audra found her way to check on Mandy by bright moonlight. "The animals will be glad in the fields," she thought and climbed back into bed. As Audra dropped off into sleep, grey squirrels — or something — tossed fir cones onto the shake roof. Chase has told her, "The best thing to do is take a shotgun to them. They wipe out birds, they wipe out rabbits and they'll get your cat and your chickens and live to brag about it. Meanest critter on the coast. Blow off the heads if you get the chance."

Audra sat up in bed and said softly, "Better get going, you pesky varmints, I've got a gun." Barnett shoved at her hip. Maybe "You better get going, I've got a gun" is all he heard.

The hours are starting to add up. Audra can't keep her hands quiet or even leave the kitchen where she stands, smoking and making pieces of hard rye toast with spoonfuls of peanut butter. She could care less if fat drips into breast tissue in a cancerly way. At the end of their first week of marriage, as once again she served the coffee, this time in her underwear, this time from a secondhand blue and white Corning pot, in a lowlight log kitchen, Barnett said confidentially, "Have you noticed that men tend to just pass over or ignore your breasts?"

Audra is about five months into the Mandy pregnancy, nauseous from the time she goes to sleep till the time she goes to sleep and trying to make it through a correspondence course, *Introduction to Calculus*. Maternity wear is two of Barnett's better plaid shirts and one pair of his grey flannel dress pants. There's a chance she looks stylish, but Audra fears she resembles a rodeo clown. Yet another perm will not take to her hair.

Barnett is supposed to be salvaging wood from a barn across

town. But he shows up for dinner with Chase and Chase's bride-to-be, the school teacher from Merrit. Jane is a bushy redhead in a Mexican blouse, pale with bright embroidery around the very scoop neck, and a thin skirt you can't help but look through. There's underwear under there but so what. Those three drink tequila. Audra would like to drink tequila and throw up for good reason instead of for this nagging kind of reason that won't even come right out and be vomit. Jane's fingers remain calm around Chase's knee.

After making and serving dinner and leaving the dishes, Audra cannot stomach their cigarette smoke and goes to bed. She is reluctant to leave those three alone but longs to overreact to some indiscretion – a laugh too loud – or what she will find of them in the morning: legs, couch, ash. She has never been so out of control, with the obnoxious throb in her head, in her stomach, at the top of her fattening legs where already this baby presses on sciatic nerves giving her one sleeping position to choose from.

Barnett in bed late, chemicals plug his pores. "You were certainly everybody's idea of a bitch tonight."

"Are they still here?"

"They went out for hospitality. They thought they'd try to get a room at the SPCA. Better food and the folks there talk nice to you. Listen, Joe. Get it together or fuck off."

Would banging her head against the cobblestones behind the woodstove signal the baby to escape, to make a run for it?

Murray says twenty years ago plenty of elk used this part of the island. With the zeal of an eyewitness, he points out it was not simply a case of overkill. "In 1973, they gave out 10,000 licenses and those idiots only got a thousand elk and they could've taken anything – bulls, cows, calves, anything. But by late summer, early fall, the bulls are in rut. That's when you see the animals get into trouble. They'll get so interested in wallowing they'll drown in muck before they can pull themselves out and back on safe ground. One October, when the telephone company rewired the whole south coast, I was mushroom-picking at the back of my property and came on two bulls in a stand of red alder. Those animals were just lying there – pretty fresh – all hung up in leftover phone wire. Must've suffocated, the wire wrapped in their antlers and then tighter around their necks just below the mandibles. Deep track-gouged marks in the ground, saplings uprooted."

Five hours past when Barnett and Mandy should have been at least somewhere. Chase is on his way to stay with her or go out after them, whatever she wants. The RCMP have been phoned but don't want to look into whatever this is. "How 'bout we leave it until late afternoon, ma'am, and give them the chance to show up on their own. I do need to ask: Did you and your husband have some sort of marital dispute? Well, if so, give him time to cool off, maybe consider offering your apologies." The comfort of strangers through wires tangled taut.

Last spring, they tried the drive to Chase and Jane's cabin using the same logging-road-and-trail route. Audra knows about wrong turns because they took one that day and they'd take it again, the signs to head that way were so convincing. It must have been a deer trail or hiking path.

    They came to a calm river and found a family of five camping in a semi-permanent lean-to, swimming, cooking stew over a campfire in round river rocks. Clean smoke. These people had erected a six-foot cross of white beach pine at the side of their building. The children – three girls of similar size, all around six – ate red bell peppers and stood naked in cold water to their knees. A shaved dog stretched beneath low branches; some Arctic breed, maybe a husky, fighting low heat. The tanned woman wore cotton underpants that covered her tight stomach, and a jogging bra, too big, the panel at the back stained yellow. The man wore coveralls without a shirt, and, Audra could see beyond the waist, without underwear.

"Uh-oh. Time warp," Barnett said to Audra. Audra worried for the safety of the children.

"Sorry," Audra called out. "I guess we took the wrong turn." Mandy listened and watched and said, "Go for swimming pool?" Barnett stared into the scene, not putting the truck in reverse, not talking, making no move. The man pointed across the river and up the steep bank and called back calmly, "If you can make it, the road's just beyond those poplars. If you can make it. Give them some room, little girls," as if, no question about it, they would put it in four-wheel drive, ford the river and climb the bank.

The water too deep, the incline too sharp, the engine wet and unwilling to turn over, the truck and all involved got stuck.

"Give it some time to dry out," the man said, sounding like a 45 playing at $33\frac{1}{3}$. "Why don't you give it some time and then try again."

"There's coffee," said the woman, in a voice just as thick.

For two hours, barely a word was exchanged. The children played, naked and gleeful, river water coursing down their backs and over their lovely tummies. The woman would leave what she was doing – baking bread or bannock or biscuits – wade in her underwear, kneel and submerge to her neck and then walk out without so much as a shaken shoulder or turned head. It was hot, but only May hot, and Audra wondered about the nature of an act meant for July.

The man spent the whole time building a miniature sailboat from windfall. Breaking, bending, lashing small branches, drinking coffee. The stew was potato and onion and squirrel. He framed a tiny grey hide with long twigs and white thread and, with bits of dark flesh still under his fingernails, raised it.

"All the little girls," he called out sweetly, slowly, "I have the boat set to launch. We're ready to sail, little girls."

Audra looked up Roosevelt elk and then looked up deer, stags, hinds, and harts and tried to make some sense of what she was sure had been a sign. There was a story about Celtic burial grounds where skeletons were found in marl layers in the beds of dry pools.

> *The creatures, with their terrific overweight of horn, had approached the treacherous edges of these pools, fringed round with soft turf, and the water covered with a mass of Potamogeton, chara, and other weeds; they must have plunged in head-first with no hope of escape.*

Damn the Celts and their dark. What about good news.

Each evening, Audra goes back to the clearing where she saw the elk. She can't find any sign. *Lithe, tense, aloof and incredibly fleet.* "Probably took off looking for girlfriends," Barnett said. "Lock up your daughters." Murray thought there'd been a bull sighting the year before in the park. "Thought he'd be poached by now."

Just to feed it by hand.

This evening, though, she'll stay here in Mandy's room and wait for Chase. He's coming the back road to look for signs of them. On the phone, fraught, Audra told him about the turn to the river, the steep bank, the wet motor, the family.

It is dark when Chase comes into the cabin and places a pale and sleeping Faye on Audra and Barnett's bed, tucks the comforter around her curled shoulders. He takes a half-inch of cold cigarette and the coffee cup from Audra's left hand, the piece of hard toast from her right. He kisses her forehead first, pulling limp curls back to do it, and then kisses her cheek and presses his smooth face against it, rubbing his hands up and down her back, massages her neck.

Nightgown still on.

"I know everything you're thinking. But fear not, Aud-one. He's gotten stuck somewhere, that's all. Happens to everybody." The smell of Jane's apricot soap on Audra's face.

Audra slides between her child's sheets. They are covered with fat primary numbers in primary colours. The cat strolls in to chew Mandy's blanket; Audra listens to squeaking acrylic fibres. She thinks, "He could've at least remembered that."

II
Round River

Round River

The bunkhouses where we slept were so cold that the words froze as soon as the men spoke. The frozen words were thrown in a pile behind the stove, and the men would have to wait until the words thawed out before they knew what was being said. When the men sang, the music froze, and the following spring the woods were full of music as odd bits of song gradually thawed out.
       Paul Bunyan Swings His Axe, *Dell J. McCormick*

Duff and Peter sleep at opposite ends of a cedar house that creaks in temperature changes and morning-after sun. Constructed by soon-to-be-forsaken Japanese boatbuilders in the 1930s, the house is watertight and slightly haunted; it would float if need be. I'm wearing Duff's Navy sweater and sipping last night's coffee   *It was so cold that when Hot Biscuit Slim set the coffee out to cool it froze so fast the ice was hot*   assessing what nightfallen deer have done to my plot. I thought they were supposed to stay close to their young this time of year.

With only a shard of moon to light the leaves, they picked clean anything with chlorophyll; they have chewed not quite to ground level, leaving opaque white stems like young bone rough cut and shredded. Exposed and garbled so early in the year, the shoots will not come back; late frost threatens and will take what's left.

I am reminded – it's early, I slept poorly and not for long – of the time I left my turtle on your bedroom floor. You were a late teen; I was eight. While the Rolling Stones huffed and puffed "Brown Sugar" above the Hoover, your bare foot twisted down. A vacuuming mishap the family later mythologized and excused. You scraped crushed viscera from deep pile with infinite coral fingernails, showing not remorse, not disgust, but glee. I looked at what I imagined to be tiny bones – do turtles have bones? – pulverized despite carapace. You incited my hysterical moment. "Ha, ha, your turtle's dead!" I felt liable; I should have cleaned that bowl weeks ago.

But it wasn't me who left the gate open last night; I didn't let the deer in. I have suspicions. It's early in the year and there will be other crops. ("I guess I'll buy you another one," you conceded.) I walk the high, hard road of Inchcape Lane in search of hotter coffee, better spirits risen above favouring barbiturate memory.

Canada geese zigzag, sucking slugs the size of plantains off the driveway. The cemetery at the corner has been stormed by dogstooth violets, loose primula and trillium. Photographers-in-training come to take their best shots, implying the day of the week with the angle of staged sunbeam filter. It's lambing season. My neighbours want me to hold a baroque nipple to the muzzle of yet another day-old struggler. I can't muster an excuse since even a child would feel important given this role.

If I said the lamb was pitifully passed over by its aged mother, who had the filthy, matted fleece of a heavy smoker, you'd say I was trying to make a point about maternity. It was, I'm not. Don't blow this up; I just don't want to nurse.

This season, every third newborn needs human intervention. My neighbours are disappointed in me. "Is there something else I can do to help? Show me how to fix up bottles." That makes me the second mammal in one day to reject this flagging thing. I'm worried about some morning when I venture out across Inchcape Lane, walk through the neighbours' decrepit latticed gate, past drooping deer fence and piles of rotting chicken shit and come upon my woolly foster. Sturdy, shorn, and picturesque, that sheep snubs me and bleats, "You're not my real mother."

The static of what you're not saying crackles with superiority; you always do this. All I mean is, I do not care to bottlefeed livestock that will not subsequently greet me in a grateful way. I'd use the word "behooved" but you wouldn't laugh.

Loose buckles click on Duff's boots as his body bulldozes through sheep-shit runoff, and spring rain muck. "You folks need a wet nurse, I'm your man." Shaved and alert. The sleeves of his shiny workshirt are rolled up prematurely given the hour; the hair on his forearms appears too fine to deflect even this anemic sun. The polestar is the buckle on his belt: one long-handled axe chopping across another, both suspended in faux-bronzed time to form a long-limbed X. Centre of attraction.

I'm not aroused by men who dress, smell, or cook like me. I am helplessly seduced by men who think like me, but quickly put down and off. I'm certain that in our two years I have not messed with this man's style. Sometimes the discrepancy between his and mine equals our primary sexual motivation, so I harbour it. "Keep the bottles coming," says Duff urgently. "This one'll make it, guaranteed."

I met him at a Bilston Creek Ratepayers Association meeting. We convened on a Tuesday night in Duff's living room, some wealthy-already landowners, one or two pillars who never miss a meeting of any denomination. Duff invited the band chief and she came with her twelve-year-old daughter. I was renting a toppling farmhouse just inside the reserve, on Buccaneer Cove, and I wanted to know how long to count on waterfront and cheap, white-woman rent. Ignorant and urban, I didn't know (a) renters aren't ratepayers, or (b) the reserve is federal.

The municipality told Duff to get a permit to fall trees on his own land, that was his stake in the meeting. He'd been logging in the Burdock Valley for forty years. His hand-hewn voice, "My father and his brothers planted some of that timber half a century ago. Now those bureaucraps figure they're gonna call the shots? No bloody way." Duff was at the meeting, he says now, in search of a woman like me. I take that to mean wordy and slightly soured.

The daughter spent all evening trying to sit next to Peter, Duff's eighteen-year-old son. Peter's long hand spread firmly across his own knee, keeping it steady, unable to swerve into hers accidentally or otherwise. They didn't speak. I watched him, his smooth face. Small eyeglasses – gold wire frames – made him look like the only one in the room who'd read a book start to finish. As the chief went out the back door, holding hands with her bewildered girl, she said to Duff, "The rhubarb loaf was good."

I stayed to drink beer in Duff's kitchen, along with a local backhoe operator and the sheep-shearing son of an ailing landowner. I admired Duff's mixing bowls, nesting pale yellow ceramic, deep, chipped, stained from too many nights soaking in the sink. And the poster-sized print hanging on smooth, dark boat-wall next to the stove: a broad team of sepia oxen, *Skidding Spars Along the Fraser River, New Westminster, 1925*, an achromatic man self-conscious beside them, posing. "This picture is you?" I asked.

Duff came close beside me. His cheek the victim of Loggers' Small Pox, mean dimples mark where someone put a calk boot to his face. (Who could get so mad?) "That's a shot of my uncle Ross the hooktender. My dad's big brother. See? He's the one hooking up that ugly beast in front, getting the turn of logs going.

"Here's lesson one: these days, I'm minus the Grade-A beef, but I'm still called a hooktender. Like he was. . . . Cancer."

You remarked about one of my more long-term boyfriends – like Duff, an Older Man – that he, quote, gave you the creeps. He hugged you once, after we'd all walked the Brunette River, and you'd found him damp and sour. Perversion was implied. But Duff would not give you the creeps; he wouldn't give you anything. It takes the right questions to get something out of Duff. You never ask questions.

I eased into an intimate moment with the poetry of a hard sell: "Those bowls have seen many a loaf of bread." Duff turned away to ask the backhoe guy about easements and access roads. I pursued it. "Are you the baker-man, or does your son do the cooking?" It was as if a screwdriver had pried open the family trunk. He turned back to me, sidled in behind the cluttered counter. Pleasant, close, willing.

"Lesson two: those" – he moved the bowls to a ledge high above the sink – "belonged to my sister, Beatrice. Up to last spring, she came every Wednesday to do the baking, and every

Sunday to watch nature programs on the colour TV. My son Pete called her Hot Biscuit Slim, after Paul Bunyan's cook. She put up with it, knew he respected her. . . . Also cancer." Duff offered me another Lucky and pulled out a chair at the table, scraping softwood floors with his flirt.

The young sheep are hungry and abstracted. Duff's technique reminds me of how he starts the older of his two Pioneer chainsaws: feet a wide parallel, arms suddenly pumped larger than life, an instant of focused prayer and pre-surge stillness, and the lamb latches on with astounding force, knocking Duff off-balance to one knee and sending that clown smile flying across his big face. In one ravaged logger hand, he cradles the lamb's narrow chin and formula runs to his elbow and drips. The bottle's done in thirty seconds. *"Next!"* Duff shouts, and sets his legs for another pull.

The erotics of this scene are not lost on me and, for the same reason I can't buy silk underwear off a hanger, I quietly retreat. But I can't go home, not with Peter there, at the house, in the kitchen, and Duff here. I require more than six hours of lousy sleep and bitter coffee to sort through the difference, if any, between cause and effect. Muck to wade through and clear.

These are the facts: last night, as we sat together at the kitchen table, the fridge shaking the floor, I permitted my hand – palm down and flat – to linger indiscreetly in the lap of Duff's son. I brought the same hand to my face and pulled it slowly, like an outlaw's bandanna, across my mouth and nose. Peter stared at his own innocent hands. Duff didn't notice, mesmerized by TV news children. During hurricanes, their mothers lash them to trees so their starving bodies won't be lost kites over Bangladesh. Long before the sportscast, Peter stood back from the table, put his hands in the front pockets of his jeans, said good night to his father, and went off to bed. What was that supposed to mean?

I bet you think this is another case of my compulsion to seduce. You believe men are attracted to me because I am as vulnerable as that soft-shelled turtle. I must be at fault because this never happens to you. You never did know how to have fun.

My attraction to Peter began with my attraction to his father, at the ratepayers' meeting. More beer and the conversation circled camp talk and the old days of logging. The evening became a wake to mourn victims of flying chokers and wire rope: fingers, limbs, severed spines and heads, a retarded boy's bloated body found and hooked off a boom. "I've seen guys walking boomsticks get dragged down by their calk boots and pulled to the bottom. Their feet tangled in weeds." Duff's right hand an artifact, a visual aid on the kitchen table, missing three fingers lost in the haulback block thirty years ago. A couple of lousy jokes about what the remaining ring finger was good at. I left Duff's kitchen around midnight. Unasked, Peter walked me out: "Those Civics'll run forever," he said, admiring my round and rusted vehicle.

Deer in the yard that night, too. A young doe stood with her front legs up the trunk of a crabapple, hind legs long and delicate, pale neck extended; she was determined to anoint that huge black nose with new growth. Interrupted, her ears flicked with our presence; she bounced over loose barbed wire and down the creek bank, sprang into the cover of deep, moon-shiny green Oregon grape. The frogs shut up for a minute. "Nice to meet you," said Peter, and he shook my hand, hunched one shoulder to his smooth face. The moon so bright, I didn't need high beams to guide my twisted way home.

I returned to Duff's house the next afternoon, uninvited, just as Peter arrived from school (a year of grade eleven Duff says did more harm than good). Peter got two Luckys from the house and we sat on the rock wall, next to the hollow boatshed, soaking simple sun and waiting for Duff. I could have used some imagination, but I asked about school instead.

"All I need's a mistake eraser," he said and scuffed gravel over a spotted slug making for the pansies. "Then I'd do okay."

"A what?"

"Didn't you ever read Paul Bunyan when you were a kid?" This was not a rhetorical question; he waited for my answer and took off his glasses when I said, "I don't think so."

"Johnny Inkslinger invented the mistake eraser," he started.

"I know about the blue ox, Babe or whatever. And about Paul Bunyan being really big. Johnny what?"

"Okay." Like telling a Bible story to a Buddhist. "Johnny Inkslinger was Paul Bunyan's sort of accountant. He had this magic pen that never ran out because a hose went between it and a big barrel of ink. Ten gallons."

"So he invented the fountain pen, too?"

"Anyway. Inkslinger wrote so fast the barrel had to be filled every couple of days. Pretty expensive. Bunyan told him to cut down. So Inkslinger quit dotting his i's and crossing his t's and that way he saved nine gallons of ink a week."

"This eraser thing. How did it know what was a mistake and what wasn't?"

"It was this big rubber sponge he just rubbed over a page of numbers. It erased the mistakes and left all the rest. It just worked, you're not supposed to know why. I could use one, that's all." Peter took our empty beer cans and started toward the house.

As his father drove up in the has-been pick-up, Peter fired aluminum at the windshield. I could see Duff behind the wheel, laughing. He got out and kicked dirt on Peter's white sneakers, shouting some family joke about Social Services coming to take the delinquent into custody. He slammed the truck door and wrapped an arm around Peter's neck. If Peter was a black Lab, he would've been yapping and jumping up and pissing on bent fenders.

I thought, How can they do this all the time and not get empty?

This might interest you: Johnny Inkslinger was the only one in Paul Bunyan's camp who knew how to cure sickness of any kind. He helped Babe the Blue Ox the time she swallowed the hot stove: built a scaffold and sent six men down her throat on ropes to investigate. You would probably say that Inkslinger represents a healer in the culture of logging camps, some sort of maternal figure, and go on to suggest that women like you, inasmuch as you counsel the pre-adolescent bereaved and abused, occupy a position totemically similar. That, I think, is bullshit. See, Johnny Inkslinger led the way with his lantern until they all reached the door to one of Babe's stomachs. You don't have a lantern. Nor could you lead the way if you had one because you are not Johnny Inkslinger. You are the hot stove behind the door.

I moved into Duff's house within a couple of weeks. Duff claimed sick leave for the first time since he'd lost his fingers. We trucked my old mattress off to the dump. Worldly goods: my red leather armchair, a dozen crates of books, my Japanese flowering maples, and the piano, all fit into a sunroom (once an add-on sewing room) overlooking the vegetable plot. We tapped walls in search of suitable studs to bear the burden of Grandmother's mirror.

When Duff went back in to camp, I spent long mornings with coffee at the kitchen table, thinking about writing songs, knitting sweaters, stripping tables; thinking about rare perennial seeds to sow in egg cartons. Frozen spots of myself thawing out. I taught piano in our home to sad and scabby kids from the trailer park next to the reserve, though none had their own instruments.

I drank beer, gained weight beyond my favourite jeans, read Paul Bunyan, and attended more ratepayers' meetings with Duff. The reserve got the waterpipe extension and started making culture-saving plans. Taxes on the huge parcels of Bilston Creek property went up forty percent; the ratepayers' membership rose to one hundred people. A huge hand-lettered sign outside the community hall announced the date and time of meetings, another one covered a prominent section of chainlink fence around the new Arbutus View Golf and Country Club.

For Duff, the issue had gone past tree-falling rules and authority. He didn't want to saddle Peter with land he couldn't subdivide – or even hand log – without paperwork and somebody's permission. Peter aspired to do mill work and till an abundant garden; nothing else moved him, and Duff feared Peter wouldn't make the taxes at this rate, let alone support a family. "Pete's going to think he's pissing off my memory if he ever has to unload. He'd walk away from it before he sold the whole works to city strangers. The bureaucraps can't understand our situation. Let the boy sell an acre or two when the time comes." At each meeting, Duff got louder. Women turned to consult their husbands while he got it all off his chest.

I climb behind Duff's house into meadowland thick with stumps, buttercups, and magic daisies; two arbutus – crazy woman trees – tangle and scratch blue sky; I know why Duff spared these. Resting permanently atilt beneath one is the white and red skiff Peter sailed as a child. Duff taught him to patrol the ponds, checking for nesting geese and contamination, beaver fever in the water supply. Peter brought me up here my second spring to show off the clean face and shaky knees of the latest calf. Its mother spurned my carrot, suspicious of handouts. I leaned against the boat's starboard side, Peter propped his elbows on a rotting paddle. The two cows watched us watch them.

"I used to pretend I was working for Paul Bunyan and I was on the Round River. It supposedly flowed in a circle and I believed in it. I must've gone around the pond a hundred times a day scouting stands of timber for the crew to fall. Anyway, I kept the geese away."

"Did you read anything else as a kid?"

"Do Dad's *Playboy*s count? I skipped Huck Finn and them, read everything Steinbeck wrote when I broke my leg and my ankle a couple winters ago. Gust of wind picked me up and threw me in a ditch. To tell the truth, reading makes me want to go to sleep. I didn't have a lot of time when I was a kid. Lots of projects.

"Like one whole hot summer, I used to ride my tricycle down the road to the graveyard, going really slow and making air brake noises like my Uncle Harper's White. I climbed the little fence – way too low to keep out kids – and picked the church flowers like I was falling trees. For my mom. By the time I got that big old White up the hill and down the driveway, what was left of the flowers was trashed and dirty and she never got any.

"It was a good time, being a kid. Too busy to get all fucked up about life. Too much air or something. I loved my mom. I always thought my dad was okay. We only ever had one fight and that's because I didn't do the dishes. Hear that? Quails laughing."

They placed Paul Bunyan's mirror on the ground with the glass side up and piled dirt around the edges. In a short time the mirror looked like a beautiful little lake. The trees along the edge could be seen in the mirror as if it had been real water.

You remember that one August; the heat was unbearable. It was so hot where we lived, the pumpkins in our rose garden started out the day as golden trumpet blossoms and finished off the day all carved up and burning like jack-o-lanterns; by midnight, the garden grinned fire from ear to ear.

There was nowhere to stay cool. Our hoses shed skin like snakes and slithered into the shade of wilted laurel. Our terrier dug a hole beside the birdbath straight down to the Swiss Alps; when she came back in September she knew how to yodel.

Our mother played bridge each afternoon under the shade of someone else's chestnut tree, soaking up dark Navy rum and Coke and chain-smoking Black Cat cigarettes. You were responsible for keeping my little body cool at home, out of the blistering sun. The family story is that's the summer you taught me to recite poems. The Summer of the Perpetual Couplet, we called it. You remember.

Our mother had painted the cement floor in the basement a rich blue to conceal wood bugs and off-season seepage. *The snow, instead of being white, was bright sapphire blue. Loggers still call it the Winter of the Blue Snow.* There was a case of stockpiled Heinz baby food, the jars antiseptic, small and sealed; I had matured beyond mush. Each afternoon, once our mother had driven off, you removed my cotton shift, my two-piece bathing suit, my pink rubber thongs, and had me lie straight out across the cold blue floor. I asked for my thongs back; you said No.

I spit out vegetables down my chin but allowed you to spoon-feed me apple sauce and strained bananas. You were naked, too, but never did lie on that icy floor. At fourteen, early periods caused narrow breasts to emerge and slope before your long straight legs and non-existent waist could curve and bend and fill you out. When I clamped my lips together and turned my cheek to the concrete, unable to stomach any more, you set a Naugahyde chair before an etched, bevelled, immovable mirror – Grandmother's – and had me sit deep in your lap to learn poetry.

You kept the lights off. Sunlight barely made it past the heat-seeking beefsteaks against the high windows. But we could see ourselves. I could make out the brown beauty mark over your top lip. One day I would learn:

> In what distant deeps of skies
> Burnt the fire of thine eyes?

The next day, sticking bare again to your bare lap, I would recite the previous day's lesson and then go on to:

> Whose woods these are I think I know
> His house is in the village, though.

See, I can still do it.

I didn't sleep nights. The humidity, mosquitoes; kids down the street, allowed to stay up and play, shouted rules to each other. Under a thin cotton sheet, I practised lines learned in the basement that day. I did not want to know the punishment should I not achieve the assigned rhyme (you slapped my face once for chewing gingersnaps too loud). I spoke the lines in whispers at dinner, during cool bathtimes, at breakfast, in church, while commercials were on TV. The death of poetry.

> Gave the clothing of delight,
> Softest clothing woolly bright.

Despite my obvious exhaustion, our mother was thrilled with the job you were doing. She never knew of the basement ritual and dismissed my sticky, swollen eyes as seasonal, a transient allergic reaction. You said I would thank you. My teachers, you bragged, would call me a prodigy. *The men put green sunglasses on Babe in winter so the snow looked green, like nice green grass. She ate and ate and grew fat and healthy again in no time at all.*

Duff's fields are refuge, a last resort to calm community livestock endangered by flood, fire, and farmhouse disharmony. Spring is so early here. The firemen's grumbling hives perch high in Duff's field and, back in January, the honeybees floated down to suck chilled snowdrops.

Duff has found me in the swarming meadow, amid invasive golden broome and warring birds, up behind his house. He smells of sour formula, last night's Luckys, and Ivory soap. We are so high up I can see all of Bilston Creek, Buccaneer Bay, the city, the Swiss Alps, last winter's blue snow, and the coming summer's yellow drought.

In bed last night we drank tea and shared the newspaper; geese honked territorially along nightfall. Duff, for the first time in two years, did not bring my hand to his pocked face and kiss the palm. He doesn't sit next to me on this crumbling and infested cedar stump though there is room. He removes his shirt, spreads it flat over shot dandelions and coarse new grass, and lies down. The belt buckle glows on his grey belly-hair; I've never seen grey hair so thick. To rest my face there.

"You'd make a good mom," I say.

His eyes are closed. "My father used to ramble on about the pros and cons of chainsaws," Duff begins. "He knew their value, of course, but he remembered the times before them, too. 'There's nothing like the sound of a crosscut saw on spruce.' He said things like that."

An explosion resounds below and the ground stirs; they are blasting granite, preparing the ground for a 24-hour casino on the reserve. *So Babe the Blue Ox pretended she was an earthquake.* Duff waits for the air to stop shaking, but it persists. "I hope they know where the runoff's going. They better keep it out of these ponds or the feds can give me two inches of water and unlimited use." Aftershock.

"I've tried to show Peter there's more to life than big dirty machines and falling trees. I will not discuss Pete's mother except to say she was stronger than a D-4 Cat in everything except her heart; it was her heart that beat her, if you can see what I'm saying. She left Pete way too soon, that's all you need to know. Yes, he's twenty years old. But Pete needs women around who don't resent being mothers to him and sisters to him and good friends to him. My job's big enough. You're not doing yours, and I want you to make up your mind. Do you want the job or don't you? And also, if you value what's yours around here, you'll keep your hands off my boy."

So it wasn't me who left the gate open last night, and I did not let the deer in.

I put a blade of new grass in my mouth. Someone's playing harmonica in a protected bay; there is blues talkback, bits of song. Or bees.

Thanks to you, *For sweetest things turn sourest by their deeds, Lilies that fester smell far worse than weeds* is all that comes to mind. You think I will fall apart, slip comfortably into my victim robes, maybe call you and wonder aloud how this could happen, what went wrong, will this never stop. I'll hang on your professional opinions like a first-grader. You will talk about family romance, models, group dynamics and systems, bring up our mother's ambivalent maternity, and blame her substances or lack of them for the mistakes I make, careful not to paint over my complicity.

Duff sits up, his back a large map before me. "My father used to say, 'Hand falling was so quiet,' but I've done it too and I know there's no difference."

The harpsichord shrill of varied thrush.

"The bounce of timber hitting dirt is loud no matter how it was cut or who cut it."

Dressing for Hope

Norma says she'll borrow the truck from Pavo so we can get the hell out of Hope for the day. She bounces on the end of the bed a couple of times, then takes the lid off my Coleman cooler, hunting good stuff for a hangover, something loaded with Bs. I smell feta cheese and wet onions because they gave me the room farthest away from the ice machine; the stripper gets the ice machine, we get rooms overlooking Harley-land. Like musicians don't sleep, or think, or merit clean air. What are we, plywood?

After work last night – mine in the lounge, hers in the cabaret – we came up here and ate my Greek salad, drank my Yukon Jack with fresh limes, and waited for pay-TV to get explicit. There was one good bit where some redhead visited her boyfriend in jail. Under her sensible pleated skirt she wore bikini underpants with strings on the sides. Her long fingers pulled the little bows; she masturbated for her con-man through Plexiglas. We're gonna get some, for a joke.

I offer Norma my fieldberry yogurt, point to the spoon on top of the television. We left the set on all night, so the spoon will be warm in the already limp yogurt. She comes back to bed, leaving the lid off the cooler, but who am I to pass judgement on niceties? I'm the one who can't face the chambermaid to give her my dirty towels. Every morning I shout at her through the door, "I'm okay." I'm sure the maid would just as soon stay out of our wing. Imagine what she finds in Pavo's room. Just in the ashtrays.

Norma told me some things about Pavo Dorado last night, some worldly stuff about Vietnam and why he wears satin tights and black boots with silver lightning bolts just to sing Willie Nelson tunes. Why he gets his hair dyed blond and permed and tied in a gigantic pony tail with a miniature Confederate flag. Why he drawls when he's from Seattle. His real name. Norma repledged her love for him, even though, as we spoke, Delphine the Hooker of Hope was probably doing that thing with the toothbrush to him.

Norma and Pavo are one half of the Southern Sky Band. No one knew we'd all be playing the Hope Hotel at the same time. Company on the road is a bonus. I would be happy to give my agent the fifteen percent if I could be guaranteed company, a family unit; don't make me watch TV until six in the morning all by myself.

Norma likes the road. She has nine brothers and sisters and never had her own room. The novelty wore off, I'm guessing, since this is Friday and that makes four nights she's raided my cooler and four mornings she's woken up on the end of my bed.

There's James Taylor on *Sesame Street*; some blue puppet's playing tuba. I wonder if he still does heroin.

"Isn't that Carly Simon on tuba?" says Norma.

"Sure looks like her. The lips."

I'm still wearing pantyhose from last night. I open the curtains and make coffee on the windowsill; Norma can't believe I grind my own. The fact that I use Jamaican beans makes her kick her feet up and down like she's laughing, only she's too hung over to laugh. I indulge in the morning. I've read somewhere that expensive coffee is easier on your system, less caffeine; they don't use DDT in Jamaica. I take my cup of coffee into the bathroom and lock myself in.

A bang on the door as she leaves. "Ten minutes, Miss Hepburn."

Summertime in this shallow valley is like being wedged between the wall and the couch. Once you've looked at one green lake from a Ford Econoline, you've seen the province. Tourist dust gives the leaves a matte finish. CN tracks racing the river make you want to be down there instead of up here on the shimmery pavement looking for a place that sells hard ice cream. I considered writing a book once, a profile of this highway: *The Rest Stops Don't Smell So Bad in Winter*. I might still do it.

We're headed to a café past the lake, up the river, out of town in Pavo's truck. Norma wants to go because she had a summer job there when she was eighteen: an adventure, the way she goes on about it. She's twenty-eight. You'd never guess, though she is starting to look a little old around the eyes. She talks about that summer the way my sister talks about Europe. My sister came home with lederhosen, a cameo ring, a dozen colour slides of the David; Norma still has a blue ribbon won at the Ashcroft Stampede's Young Miss Goat-tail Tying Contest. She believes she was transformed into an adult with a world view that summer.

"Patsy Cline has to have the most honest voice ever, I don't care what kind of music." Norma is shifting, double-clutching, tinkering with the no-draft, steering, smoking, inserting tapes, cracking cans of beer, drinking. She sings along to the Jordanaires' part in "Faded Love."

"Maybe," I say. "But I'm wondering if she ever actually watched the 'mating of the dove.'" I sing acoustic guitar arpeggios just behind the beat. Norma pumps the brake to signal she's laughing.

Pavo has painted a naked Indian woman onto the back doors of his truck, only enticing tailgaters, in my opinion. And sure enough, a horn blows three times behind us. Guys in hats pass us;

they hoot and wave and lean on each other and out at us. "Never mind," I tell myself with my mother's voice.

We sit outside the café until Norma has heard the very end of her song: "Lu-huuuuuuuv"; my face out the window, turned up to the sun to work on what my father calls a barroom tan.

"Never mind" what the café looks like on the outside, the inside says it all. This is no place to bring hangovers. No food anywhere, per se, only the linger of it in the air, on the windows, under the tables. A pair of handsome blonds greets us in the middle of the room. Tidy and brown in minimalist shorts, they are aligned in some way with Norma. As if they've known this moment of sexual gravity would occur. Norma has yellow hair, too, just like these guys.

I am betrayed and cast out, a social nova. I sit on a stool, my back to the counter, and watch a truck head for the canyon, taking a run at it like a lean little boy on a long diving board. Another few miles and it will be in slow motion, climbing into wild blue, then hurtling down the other side, shooting past the pull-out sign at the bottom.

I catch up in the next room where all the blonds are holding pool cues and bottled beer, smooth-skinned warriors with tall spears and tiny shields. The three of them watch each other bend over.

"They want us to shoot the river," Norma whispers hard and straight into my ear. All I can see is white around her eyes.

"Shoot it with what?" A radioman on a distant kitchen counter took a course to babble about ideal highway conditions.

"They've got three inner tubes. And some coke. We can share. Let's."

They drop me out front of the Hope Hotel; we are diagonal where the signs say parallel. Back where we started so abruptly? Someone has slapped a happy-face sticker over the Indian woman's crotch on Pavo's truck. When Norma shifts gears down the road, black exhaust hides everything but that.

There is a pink message pushed under my door and the phone shrieks and throbs. RED ALERT. THE CITY. My high school sweetheart/first love Reg is calling. Outside, a giant Harley idles over our conversation like a ticked-off grizzly. From the end of the bed I can see into the mirror, Reg cradled under my chin like when we were indulged teenagers hogging the phone. My toes still remember the hours of stamping around icy street corners, tempting each other with long looks: earth-treading. For six years we did that. We are both thirty now. He is a few hours and a straight line away by Pacific Coach Lines and needs to see me. He is getting married, or thinks so, and needs to see me first. It has been twelve years and he needs to see me. My mother told him where.

He sounds the same; I am not the same, the mirror makes that clear, but how can we be sure until we have a look at each other? This is the last thing I expected and the surprise arouses everything. I tell him, "There's not much left to see," I stress burnout and provide an appropriate simile, the one about the nova. When he tells me he'll know me no matter what, there's a hint of desire in his voice, and he says, "See you soon," just as I read the pink message in my hand:

Leo called will arrive between 5 & 6.

The bed vibrates to the beat of stripper music from downstairs. Every four bars the spoon on the television rattles. The effect would be aboriginal except I know she's dancing to Billy Idol, "White Wedding."

This Leo is an ex-boyfriend's best friend. Last week, he found me by phone on a hobby farm in the Interior. I was getting away from it all, tending to some guy's cows: Stan and Rosa, the cows. I was having a road romance, too, though Stuart, the guy, took frequent two-day trips to the border and back. A cycle of some intrigue. I was alone and quiet, no one knew where I was going to be, but Leo found me. Maybe my mother told that time, too.

There was non-stop baseball on television – it seemed like a pennant race – and the Expos were involved. So I heaved the odd bale of hay at the cows, drank bottles of Kootenay Pale Ale, and watched hi-test baseball; calm men in white. Late afternoons, I'd take a beer and walk through Moose Meadow along fence posts pounded by Early Canadian cowboys, wander between volunteer silver birch.

The night Leo called, I had shared my beer with a gangly grey horse in Moose Meadow. Rain shone for a few minutes and left it sounding like barnacles at low tide. Sunlight filtered, water misted the air, and everything glistened green. It was top-lit, a fish tank with algae. Perched on a fence post, I blew into my beer bottle to see how the hoot would sound in there, drank, and blew again, trying to find a semi-tone's difference, doing a scale. This horse appeared, huge, dappled, and naked. Our eyes met, flirted. I poured beer into my hand. Nothing else feels like horse bristle on your palm. You're a little kid, tickled and scared and thrilled. We finished the beer that way, and the horse wandered off through the birch and moss, almost concealed.

Stan and Rosa big-brown-eyed me as I walked along the fence; they sensed something illicit had taken place. I dumped feed, but the cows ignored it and searched my face for clues. They'd be going through my pockets next.

"What are you doing up there for fun?" asked long-distance Leo. Leo is a renderer for an architect in the city, an adult with a job.

"Drinking with this horse. Had to listen to him go on about the old grey mare."

"So I'm coming to Hope next week to take you out for dinner."

I don't remember the last time an adult with a job took me anywhere. Maybe it was my father my last birthday, downtown at the Tennis Club. Guys with racquets stopped by our table to wipe their noses and check to see if my father was having an affair.

Leo is thirty-nine and recently separated. He plays guitar in a Legion band on weekends. Who wouldn't look forward to a meal with Leo? I've met him twice and I don't remember what he looks like so I hope he comes straight to my room when he gets here.

I hope I don't meet Reg and Leo meeting.

The future is getting crowded. I need ice.

It's three-thirty in the afternoon and Pavo is falling out of a yellowish terry cloth robe. He got to the ice machine first. From the hips up, he is in the machine, dragging a beer glass along the bottom to scoop what's left. It sounds like someone chewing sand with a microphone under his tongue. His robe threatens to reveal parts I don't want to see; the hair up his legs grows darker like a paint sample chart. Pavo heaves himself out and flips both sides of hair back, tosses it sensuously, though he doesn't know I'm there.

The stripper teeters up the stairs in ivory peau de soie high heels and a short black satin wrap speckled with sequins. A huge wedding dress flounces over her arm. Her face is haunted still by the white veil; appliquéd yellow daisies, thick black eyeliner underneath. Burgundy spikes of hair poke out. It all looks authentic, though, not a bit dime store. She will be betrothed. She passes near but exchanges nothing with Pavo. They completed the entire ritual of mating the first afternoon we were all here, went through each developmental stage between her shows that day. Now they have nothing left to give. Good manners mean nothing.

Pavo notices me. "Hey, doll-face." That's what I've heard him call Stella the stick-figure waitress in the hotel coffee shop. She has the smile of a dolphin. "Whatcha call a musician with no girlfriend?" Too-short pause. "Homeless."

"Is that it for ice?"

"Ah do believe so. Where's mah suh-weet Norma-May at?"

Talking to Pavo Dorado, just standing beside him, makes me feel like a virgin. The sex he does is nothing like the sex I do. Mine is the tricycle to his 10-speed, the daffodil to his orchid. Even the soap smell coming from him is erotic; mine is too sweet. "River-rafting?" I hear that I've made a question out of a statement and flush with low-grade shame.

Pavo strolls away without slippers. Nothing is done about securing his robe; another tiny Confederate flag where a label should be, at the neck. He walks as if he's wearing lightning bolts. "Oh." He stops and turns back to me. I'm still holding my cooler at arm's length. "Ah just had a call from Albert. He's in Chilliwack. Should be gettin' here for your first set."

"What's he doing in Chilliwack?" Three. Tonight.

"Waitin' for the rain to ease up. He's doing some kinda bicycle tour thang through the valley. Sounds like yore his final destination, little one."

"*What rain?*" I holler and drop the cooler. But Pavo has taken the last of the ice and ducked through the fire doors.

Albert is the one I want to keep one day; we barely date at this stage; the man of my dreams. I see the three of them, Reg, Leo and Albert. In a display of masculine pride and deflected passion, they clasp hands like professional athletes, teammates. I am thrown out at home; they converge.

Hair-trigger timing is doing the trick. It is my first set and Leo is upstairs in my room, sleeping off the wine he had with dinner and the imported dope he smoked on the drive here, and in my room when he arrived, and on the way to dinner, and after dinner. Leo is an adult with an addiction. Thirty-nine. Good thing he has a job. At dinner, I taught him the word "androgyny." He believes, even though it is a brand new word for him, that he loves me for that quality. A hasty decision and probably not soberly considered. Experience tells me that androgyny will be the thing to incense him a year from now, maybe even in six months, depending on how long he tolerates televised hockey, dirty dishes, and unshaved legs.

Albert understands androgyny. He's got some too, that's why he rides a bicycle. But it's raining buckets out there. The all-knowing bartender tells me the highway is closed at one low point, between Chilliwack and Hope. Albert will be a no-show.

I am two feet off the ground in the lounge of the Hope Hotel. Reg sits down against the far wall, looking like he has nothing to do with my adolescence. What with the lights so dim, the blue spot blinding even my mind's eye, I can just see a sense of him. His black hair is still curly but short now, too short. His eyebrows have joined prehistorically above his nose, and a big mustache must make it hard for him to smile. His neck and shoulders are like concrete, and humourless; we are the same height still. He looks like a cop and that will be bad for customer relations in this joint.

Already the walk-through traffic has been heavy. Bare-shouldered Harley women, oblivious to rain, pound past the stage and pretend to give the music a chance; they exit by the back door, antennae sensing danger, harassment, ill will. I admire how every step and glance is a sexual act. Their nail polish is libido. They wear tri-coloured rosebud tattoos in places I barely wash. They are as alert as I am to the mood of the room and they pass through. Blessed candles of the night.

When Norma comes in for her pre-gig scotch, I am singing Patsy Cline: *I've got your mem'ry, or has it got me?* She makes sure I see her smile at me and raise her glass in a country music salute to honest voices. She is dressed like Pat Boone's date in *State Fair*, some Debbie. Her shoes have open toes and squash heels, her skirt is full. She sits down at Reg's table as if they are old friends. I think I am glad to see she's still in one piece after the river, but it may be too soon to tell.

I try to introduce the last song of the set but Clive Joseph pinballs his way to the stage, one arm held over his head for balance, to make a request. He tries so hard to be polite, but the volume of our exchange makes it confrontation and spectacle.

"Play Tchapeeka."

"Do you mean 'The Atchison, Topeka, and the Santa Fe'?"

"No. *No*. Play Tchapeeka."

"I'm afraid I don't know that one, Clive."

"Sure you do. You know it."

"I'm afraid I don't."

"Try it anyway."

"Clive."

"*Tchapeeka! Tchapeeka!*"

"You sing it to me."

"*Tchapeeka fine time to leave me* – "

"No."

Our first close-up look at each other puzzles both Reg and me. Neither one of us gets what we expected. Instead of the eagerness and devotion we used to run on, what fires between us as I approach the table, dressed like a cross between Roy Rogers and Dale Evans, is bewilderment. Mutual. "What did I ever see . . ." brainwaves tangle in the smoke above our heads. Twinkle in his eye? Gone. Dimples? Plugged up and flattened. Even his jeans don't fit right any more. Now that he's standing, I don't think we are even the same height any more. It could be my boots, but I'd say I have two inches on him. We shake hands.

"Uh-oh. You guys know each other already." Norma sounds guilty, melodic.

Out of all the answers to pick from, the erstwhile Romeo and Juliet both choose, "We used to." I notice that when we sit down Reg's shoulder is closer to Norma than it is to me; I imagine their legs must be touching, but I'm too sophisticated to check under the table. "You two sure got friendly pretty quick." I'm not able to look at their faces; Reg examines the painted line on his beer glass, scratching at it with this thumbnail.

Norma fastens her arm around his rock shoulder. "We both worked for Northern Lights last summer."

"You played in a band?" My shock makes Reg try to laugh, but that gets clogged and he drinks a bit of beer instead.

"No," he says with prickly calm. "It was a United Church youth retreat. A wilderness camp. Outdoor experience for terminal kids. Norma and I were counsellors. Remember Reverend Morrison? It was one of his projects."

I am waiting for the punchline. We used to laugh a lot more than this. When Norma goes to the bartender to switch her order to a double, I tell Reg – too quickly – that he can't stay in my room tonight. I tell him the circumstances: "unexpected guests." I see he finds my implication that he might expect to sleep with me after twelve years offensive. "That's not what I came for," he says.

"Let me at least buy you another beer since you've come all this way," I say.

"I don't need more than one." And this is when I know the glacier is making better time than just two inches a year.

It's pretty clear, too, when he puts his jacket on in the middle of my ultimate version of "Crazy," that he's not a country music fan. He kisses Norma's mouth goodbye and lifts his hand over his head to wave goodbye to me. As he holds the door for Harley-people – they seem agitated by this gesture – I can see the rain in striped sheets against the glow of the red Exit sign. Norma is gone, too, by this time.

Leo slides shyly through the door. He asks the bartender for a big glass of water and a beer. I join him at the bar and buy myself another rum; he doesn't even try to pay.

"Good sleep?"

"When?"

"Just now. Did you have a good sleep?"

"Until your phone went off."

I mentally list all likely callers and can account for everyone except maybe my mother and Albert. "Was it Albert?"

"When?"

"Just now. On the phone. Was it a guy named Albert riding a bicycle calling from Chilliwack?" I want to slap Leo's face for answering my phone.

"It was some guy named Stuart." Leo's already on his second glass of water. There is suspense as he gulps and gulps. "He asked for you. Then he said to tell you to come and get your stuff off his property. Did I screw up?"

Stan and Rosa must've spilled the beans. "It's not your fault."

"That's what Stu said. I'm going over to play some harp with Southern Sky. You don't mind, right? Norma asked me to."

On my way upstairs after the next set, I check the ice machine, but it is empty once again. I am tempted to press an ear to the stripper's door, just to hear what she's up to with all the ice; good manners prevail. My dark room, the flutter of white dwarf music videos from the TV. Below my window, there are no Harleys. Like larks in the rain, where do they go?

"You in there?" Norma must be looking for food. Or beer. I let her in and sure enough she goes straight for the cooler. We both step back from the smell, but Norma reaches into the cheesy water and comes up with a warm can. "Want one?"

"How was the river? How's your night going?"

"Sunburn. Leo's great. Hey. I just took a call from Albert. Me and Pavo are gonna take the truck down to Chilliwack tomorrow and pick him up."

"You know Albert, too?"

"That's who I share the house with in Hesper. You didn't know that?"

"So you know all three of them?" I am yelling over TV flicker and through Harley spirits. *"What am I, plywood?"*

Clive Joseph attends my last set, but he's sleeping. The bartender plays cards with herself. Everyone else has gone to the cabaret to see Southern Sky. So I'm alone at last. I dedicate a song to the memory of the late great Patsy Cline, but it is "Silver Wings": *Don't leave me, I cried. Don't take that airplane ride.* I use a Bakersfield sound; I am being ironic.

"Quit early if you want," says the bartender.

Friday night at the Hope Hotel. The doorman at the cabaret isn't sure he should let me in, since the room is loaded. So I stand and watch, my guitar case on end in front of me, vibrating with sympathetic resonance. The band can't stop between songs, the dance floor would revolt. I recognize the glazed, puffy faces of people who were in the lounge before. They told me how much they enjoyed me, they said goodnight on their way out as if they were heading home after a lovely evening. Now, here they are, happy. Rushing the stage with free beer for the band, sending notes to Pavo with song titles spelled wrong on them, hugging each other every last chord. Even the stripper is here, in love with night, like now everybody's doing Shakespeare.

The stage is budget-sized; there's some crowding up there, a galactic cluster. Norma is radiant at her electric piano as she thuds and pounds, trying to keep up. Her hair sways against her straight back, wet around her face. She wears schoolgirl glasses, shoves them back up her nose, and looks to Pavo for cues. Leo shares her stool and microphone; a renderer.

Pavo has taken off his shirt. His chest hair is white and thick. He holds a Fender Jazz against his solar plexus. His stomach is anything but taut. The top of a star-shaped belt buckle prods his navel.

The band sounds great. Music from the spheres.

This reminds me of when my mother and father and sister would watch television at night, and I, being much younger than my sister, would lie upstairs in bed listening to them talk and laugh. I'd wait to hear my name, try to gauge whether there was love in the saying of it or not. If I heard love, I'd go down for a glass of milk. If I heard something else, I'd pull the covers over my head and make up songs about running away, riding the rails. Pavo's lightning bolts glint in amber gelled lights, Norma's glasses slip. Tonight, it feels as if I was sent to bed early.

But a frazzled Stella-the-waitress shoves a cold Heineken bottle into my hands and floats off, tray in the air. "That's from the piano player. Go on," she clicks and whistles. "You're wanted up there." She speaks dolphin.

Science Diet

The fingerprints on the window look like someone tried to get in here. A man could use a ladder to get to my balcony and, finding the sliding glass door locked, go for the window instead. He tries to move it with splayed hands, puts his whole body into quiet pressure. His fingertips, wet from the night and the climb, get good traction. But it's locked, too. His passion sours; he goes down, feet first.

I check the balcony for more clues, footprints exposed by morning sun, but find only simmer dust and Crystal Palace lobelia in terracotta pots. The fingerprints, I realize, are on the inside and my own. I must have tried to get out last night. The hard way.

Day four after a dose of cobalt or whatever they pump in, and my skin is peeling from the inside out. I can't shower; water, even tepid or cool water, burns what layers I have left. The nausea is bad company. The cat sits and watches me disintegrate. She strolls over to lick my head, cares. I could use a few hours of couch under the quilt, some drifting in and out would soothe aspects of all this. But my little brother is coming to get me for a day out in the world.

He saunters through the door like a landlord. I am sitting upright on the couch, ready, the quilt folded up like it never gets used. The cold floor is inches from where I sit: shot springs. I wonder about a new couch, where the money will come from, where I'll cut corners to afford it. I laugh, a celebration. "That sort of thing won't be necessary." What the honest nurses say when I ask for things with value in the future. That sort of thing,

He just walks right in, straight to the kitchen for beer, and comes back with one for me, too. He used to root around in my medicine cabinet when he was a teenager, looking for my weed pills, rabid for an altered state. A couple was okay with me, but any more and I felt like I used to when he'd finish the ice cream before I got my share. Now he brings joints and goes for my beer; he prospers, his life booms. He smokes, I worry for his lungs, his brain, his voice box. Already he sounds hoarse, and phone calls from him before noon are relentless throat-clearing suggestive of late Janis Joplin. Poisoned.

"So why don't you get a wig?" he begins.

"Because I want to look like a dyke and scare old people. It thrills me."

"Cool."

I'm finished my beer. He's smoking at the same time, so he's only halfway through his. I don't want to waste energy going to the fridge, I don't want to ask for service, I don't want to sit and watch him drink; I don't want to fall back to the couch if I try to get up and can't.

"I want to know where we're going," I say.

"Don't you trust me to show you a good time? When did I ever take you someplace you didn't like? You need another beer while I finish this," and he gets me one.

He had a motorcycle before, a red and black Moto Guzzi. We'd take Department of Highways ferries up and down the coast, round trips. Other bikers were spellbound and asked questions about the bike. He'd stand with his hands open around his black leather waist and give quick answers, checking his Italian boots for scuff marks. Biker chicks would look me over and think I was hot, I guess, especially if I was wearing the helmet so my hair didn't show. And I weighed more then. I was a nice straddle, I overheard that. It came from the empty cab of a Pine Ridge Milk Bread truck, first in line on the car deck.

My brother's buddies said he turned into a prick when he got that bike, but I didn't mind him that way. It made him act like he did when we were kids, arrogant and superior, the leader. All profile. Little boys are close to sexy when they have that much nerve. I hate the way it decomposes over the years; they never get over the loss, and their humour grieves for it. His buddies trashed the bike and shredded his leathers.

"At least tell me what you're driving so I'll know if I'm dressed."

"You look great. Wear what you've got on. You look hot in jeans."

"My ass disappeared the day after my tits did."

"No way. You look sacred like that. I like that look. Sixties."

"No. In the sixties everything was big, and it bounced and you could see it because everyone wore that gauze. No one was this skinny in the sixties."

"Addicts."

"True."

He takes our empty cans to the kitchen. My little brother was just a baby in the sixties, but he reminisces. He wants it to happen again, only on a bigger budget, so he can profit this time.

While he's in the kitchen, I try to make it off the couch. Mornings call for crossed fingers and visualization. Tricks. I tune in and listen to something known only as my "inner process." I see myself as a perfect human being with a fuzzy pink bubble surrounding my lymphatic system. I chant silent, irrational affirmations:

My body is balanced, in perfect harmony with the universe.
My mind and body now manifest divine perfection.
It works. I'm up and he's back.

So this one's a Nova – it was only a matter of time – all his buddies have had Novas; they all chase cars. My little brother's is painted flat black; it looks sanded down, rough. The way the back end sits up it's a predator, poised to slip beneath still waters.

"Get in from this side," he says, like that's another treat. But he's right. For the moment I'm behind the wheel, I feel potent. I look over the dash and my mind vrooms. I grab the wheel like you're supposed to and my mouth vrooms. "Sacred," I sum up.

"Shove over." He waits, standing, until I'm a passenger. He sets his jaw like a gunslinger, dips, makes an entrance.

"Is this your car or do I want to know about it?"

"Call it a loaner." He checks dormant gauges and lights a joint. "You still get those pills or do you want some of this?"

A worry skitters past: what will the neighbours do if they see me in this car with a man dressed in black and see me toke up? I wonder if the bank teller in the apartment above mine will see and ask to have me evicted. Like banks are the law. Will my neighbours petition me away for this? But that sort of thing won't be necessary, I remember. So I get the last quarter-inch he saved for me. He takes back the end and eats it.

"We're headed for the border. You got anything they're gonna worry about?"

"Do they still bust bad hair in that country?"

"Forget it. You look great."

When he turns the key and the engine kindles into a low gurgle, something starts to vibrate in him. He adjusts the mirrors redundantly and spots the delinquent he once was and climbs back in. He shifts out of Park with an open hand, manoeuvres with just the heel of it. Faint, faded tattoos glow neon from his forearm;

three needle dots between his thumb and forefinger, a shy reminder of eighteen months in the can, pulse dark blue in sync with the engine throb. He's strutting and we haven't even pulled out. He charges the road, he tailgates, runs lights, ogles and leers at civilization: little girls in white knee socks, teenagers bent over handlebars. The radio doesn't work; he pounds the dash with both hands while kids dawdle and dance through the crosswalk.

"Ease up," I suggest.

"Hey. Take off your seat belt and slide over here."

"No way."

"Come on. They'll think you snagged yourself a pretty boy with a hot car. Closer. Right on."

His arm is along the seat behind me. I lean into his shoulder, my face against his chest. He brings his hand to the back of my neck and rubs exactly three times before his arm goes back along the seat. A man's move. His shirt smells of Thai resin, leather, and deodorant soap. I am ashamed, I am a human miasma. Chokedamp. He winds his window down calmly, pretending he'd do it anyway, like it's right there in the script.

This car and my brother are the couch and quilt. I fade in and out. Twice more, he rubs my neck another three times while he drives. No radio is better.

The car, my little brother's tattoos, my hair – they pull us over at the border and make us wait through their suspicions. We all come up clean, and I can't believe it but I should know he's not that stupid, not a formal risk-taker. They ask what our business is and how long we're staying. I look at my brother for a straight answer I can live with.

"We're off to the Kiwanis Outdoor All-Breed Dog Show in Seattle. Just for the afternoon. We'll be back before dark. We're dog lovers, sir."

We're driving away from uniforms. "Really?"

"Yes, ma'am."
"Good idea."
"We need beer."

This bar knows my little brother. I'm the stranger, I get the once-over. The light change at this time of day makes me sleepy; I bet I look stoned. We sit in the darkest corner, facing the door, between the cans. Action. Service is instant, beers float in from nowhere. I taste soap on the rim of the glass and my stomach flips and threatens. I lick all round the edge and swallow fast ounces to cut the taste and fool my insides.

A thin teenage boy escorts a woman out of the ladies' can; she's dressed up like the bank teller from home. I guess at how long they've been in there by faces at their table; no one cares they're back, it's routine. After a minute, the bank teller gathers up her beer and Sportsmans and coins like provisions and finds another table without saying goodbye. No one notices, including the boy, her date. She's a marionette, lowered into the new chair; her arms flop onto the new table. Her head is released to fall forward and dangle.

My brother gets up and apologizes with a finger to the tip of my nose. "Give me ten minutes and I'll get you out of here." He bounces away, a smudge. A fresh beer is in front of me and I worry about how to get to the can and how to get out of it once I'm done. I'll wait for him to cover me.

Two men in sharp suits stand over the glow of the jukebox like cowboys at a campfire. What song takes two guys like them to pick it? Joyriding, this bar a joke they tell at the office, an anecdote for their wives years from now. They'll brag, the women aroused by nonsense.

They sit down with the bank teller. One on either side, they draw their chairs around her, into her, and make themselves into a line like they're going to watch a show or judge a contest. The bartender turns up the music and brings them each a beer. The bank teller's head is still on a slack string, nestled, now, into her chest. Power chords: "Cocaine." By the time the guy in the record finally gets to sing, the suits both have a hand under the bank teller's sweater. And they start to pull her tits, to push them back and forth and play a sort of tag with them. They lift their beers with the free hands, toast each other, and drink half, still kneading, yarding on her tits. Her head comes up but her arms can't budge. "Hey," she says. "Oh," she says, and then she smiles at me, or where I am, and waits. She glows in the dark, a puppet head with rosy cheeks on whiteface, carved sockets, sanded-down edges. They flatten her tits into her chest until the chair tips back – "Wheeee" – and then they pull her upright, their knuckles poking out, pointed hard and bony where her curves should be. And that's their finale. Ta da. They stand, drain their glasses, make sure cuffs cover their shoes. The next song is "Muskrat Love"; no wonder it took two. The bartender brings the bank teller another beer; she has to give him all her change.

 My brother blocks my view. "I'll watch the door if you wanna use the can before we head out. I'm done." He looks alert, I'll be safe. "Don't sit down in there, whatever you do," he cautions in a man voice. When I come out, he sees I've been sick but keeps quiet. His arm goes around my waist. Not a mid-marriage reflex or adolescent drape – this counts for something. "Sorry I had to leave you."

My brother wakes me up in Tacoma, parked. He hands me a not-very-cold beer from behind the seat. I'm grateful; coming to sometimes stirs me up and brings me down at the same time, but this way I have a focus for my inner process. With beer, I affirm:
 I love and accept my body completely.

I am now full of radiant health and energy.
It works. I'm awake. I am alive.

I am at Nendel's Valu Inn. There is a huge field encircled by Winnebagos, Kustom Koaches, Vanguards, pastel station wagons, late-model mini-vans with logos: Mister Ed's Pet Department Store. Stars and stripes flap from antennae, doors are wide open and canopied, aluminum lawn chairs tilt nearby. Occupied territory.

In what must be some sport's end zone, a banner stretches a shiny welcome to The Basset Hound Club of Greater Seattle. I look at my little brother for some idea, but he is looking at his watch and playing trills on the steering wheel.

"Are we allowed to be here?"

He laughs way too loud and hard. "Waddaya think, this is top secret manoeuvres or something?" He gets out. "You done with your beer?"

I toss the can into the back seat where empties wait in safety to be returned for deposit. My head whirls in the sun and upright position, but my little brother takes one step toward me and stands like a fence post waiting for the first picket.

"I thought you said Seattle. I thought you said All-Breed. These dogs are all the same. Everybody has one, everybody's walking funny."

"Pretend. As far as you know, we are at the Kiwanis All-Breed Outdoor Dog Show in Seattle. You don't want to know any more than that. This is okay with you, right?"

My little brother leads me toward a village of booths and bulletin boards where vendors achieve a homespun air of commerce with no strings attached, no ties that bind, no guarantees. Buy, sell, and trade, we're all here for the same thing.

"I'm going to be a while this time, maybe an hour."

"I'll entertain myself. Don't worry about me." He doesn't like this. When he was eleven, my mother sent him to a Christian wilderness camp. What bothered him was that I'd be alone in that house with our parents, that I'd have no back-up in case of emergency. He said he'd take his walkie-talkie and if I really needed him, somehow my walkie-talkie would be powerful enough to reach his. "The batteries are dead in mine," I said. "It'll still work," he said. He came back from camp a harder boy, toughened, I guess, by the piss-off of having to share a canoe.

He starts to walk away. "Watch yourself," I say, and he glances back at me.

I touch my hair, try to move it over the places it used to be. I run my tongue over my teeth, still amazed by how straight they are. I got braces in my mid-twenties so I would have a radiant smile for my thirties; I planned a lot of kissing for my thirties. But I spent too many years with buck teeth to accept their perfection. Sometimes I long for an overbite; I can't smile for a camera.

A tricoloured hound pulls a leash so he can smell my feet. He's ecstatic and goes up to my knees; his neck is too short to go any further, but I know he wants to. All over my legs and feet, I'm afraid he'll start to hump and I back away. He looks up for a second to see the object of his desire, and, stunned, throws his head back to yowl and bay. I am an intruder, a mailman, a critter up a tree. His ears flap, his dewlap jiggles, his stubby front legs bounce off the grass. He knows he's got the wrong gal, but he's covering with bravado. Finally, he's reined in by a sheepish man in old tweed. "He never does this." I know there will be fewer dogs among the vendors' stalls, so I enter the plywood labyrinth, hoping to disappear.

I read everything, killing time. I collect brochures, I count ribbons and explore blow-ups of show dogs. Women sit with crochet squares in their laps, poking and smiling like homesteaders. I look at their lives, tacked up and framed under plastic:

> **UNIQUE ART WORK OF YOUR PET**
> Romelia Gummig,
> Box 163, Wathena KS

There is a playpen with a toddler in it. The child resembles a polar bear in the zoo. It looks at me lazily, knows I don't belong here. Kids are telepathic. I hope it doesn't cry.

What would Romelia Gummig do with my cat, what medium? Definitely acrylic, theoretically abstract. Avant-garde. Nothing a black and white photograph couldn't say better. I take a card anyway, for the baby's sake.

The infield is a ballroom. Men and women lope by in single file, leashes taut, dogs stepping on air, a June Taylor effect. The judges stand inside this circle; they are the hub of this wheel. Cross-legged on the grass, I watch it. The dogs are radiant. Noses and tails high, deep white chests, some starred. Ears that don't give a damn who sees them swing.

A black man, must be six-four, runs with a pause, a stutter in mid-air, so his hound can keep pace and they won't trample the couple in front. He wears large wooden beads that clatter on his chest. His crotch swings heavily under satin shorts. A neck twice the length of his dog's, which is huge but short. Olympians. How many Basset hound steps to one big black man's step? I try to count, but I lose my place.

> *Tara Lara*
> Academy of K-9 Hair Design
> Master Course 640 Hours
> Student Housing
> Within Walking Distance

I try to count how long 640 hours last, to see if I'd graduate. But I lose my place there, too. That sort of thing.

There is a woman out there dressed like a cheerleader. Her legs are shiny long and smooth brown, and her calves look hard, as if she jumps up and down a lot. She moves like someone who wants to be a dancer but can't keep her weight down. In a small pink T-shirt that fits, she is large-breasted and bounces too much for this crowd. There is aesthetic imbalance; she and her dog are out of whack. The other contestants are nicely matched up, symmetrical in a master-slave diorama. This woman needs a tennis racquet at the end of her leash. Her little skirt flips like her dog's ears, and pink lace underpants show when she rounds the bend and heads up the other side of the ring. She falls behind sometimes and forces the man behind her to adjust his pace; they both look bad. The dogs do fine. Hers is the only one that has the problem of looking up. He looks at her too often; they take points off for that. But she is beautiful, who wouldn't look up? She points her toes a little with each step, so it's ballet. Her hair is long enough to fly out back. It is the same colour as her dog's hair at the base of his neck. Auburn. Her horn-rimmed glasses fall down her nose every few steps and she has to push them up with her shoulder, careful not to tug on the leash and spoil everything. She rounds the bend closest to me and I swear she winks at me and bounces her breasts a little harder. Just once, but I catch it. They are lined up and waiting to be adjudicated. She is a profile to me, right in the middle.

SINGLE DOG LOVERS ASSOCIATION
Meet other doggy people –
Showing, hunting, breeding, or just pets.
Confidential. Social functions.
PO Box 272245, Concord CA

A portable PA announces the winner of these trials, a dog named Champion Tailgate Black Bart. I want to call my little brother that from now on. The owner-operator is Orthello Dixon. The beautiful woman gets a nondescript ribbon that qualifies her for a consolation event. She looks down at her dog, he looks up at her; they shrug their shoulders and trot off. I know she winks at me; the dog looks me over.

Two ridiculously thin boys, one carrying a football, lumber past, and all I catch of their conversation is "beer garden" and "they don't give a shit at these things," so I follow. They are turned away by a fat man wearing a T-shirt that says: Tattoo-a-Pet Protection 1-800-TATTOOS. I buy a beer from him and look for a private corner. But this area, too, is a circle, a ring. I wind up dead centre and exposed. My little brother is nowhere; I watch for a flash of him in the outfield or between parked cars.

A monologue from an adjacent table entertains:

> He's married seventeen years, he's had me on the side for six, the cancer for two. You're gonna laugh at this, but sometimes I like to think of him all curled up and safe in bed with his wife. At least I know someone has their arms around him, I know he'll make it another night. And if he doesn't – well, at least she'll catch him when he falls. That picture is a comfort. I don't feel so left out. He's had it good, though. I mean having both of us and all. He prefers the retrieving breeds. I believe he hunted at one time.

> **PET CASKET AND VAULT** (Polystyrene)
> Golden Frost exterior / ivory crepe interior.
> 18 inches: $63
> ELTON STEPHENS, S. Bend IN

"I think I saw you in Woodinville two weeks back." She has changed her T-shirt. This one is blue. I wonder if she's sad because she didn't win a better ribbon. "Mind if I join you, it's really crowded in here. I got you a beer. Were you there, was that you?"

"Where was I?"

"Gold Creek Sports Club in Woodinville, the show two weeks back. Wasn't that you? Sure looked like you. I'm Mimi Brandolini."

Her fingers are long; her nails are round and hot pink like candies. We hold hands and meet. She wears a silver charm bracelet with basset hounds dangling loudly from it. There must be a dozen different ones, some just heads, others just attitudes.

"I thought you were good, Mimi, you and your dog."

"Thank you, you're kind. We do our best. It's all for Frank, really, he's the one who relies on it. He loves the shows." But there's no ring on the lovely hand around her beer.

"Your husband?" I can't look at her for this part.

"Frank? Ha. No. My dog. Sorry." Her glasses slip when she laughs; I watch her bracelet flash when she presses them back up her nose. "Champion Iceman Frank Mahovlich. I guess you could call him my significant other, but he's Frank the dog to me." She's wistful. She plays her beer can like a tiny Caribbean steel drum.

"Mimi?"

"Oh, I'm sorry. Frank's bitch passed away earlier this week. I thought it would be good for us, to be back in the saddle again, you know. But, what with the puppies – "

"You've got puppies?"

She looks up at my sparkle and glitters a little herself. She touches my hand again. She smells of lavender and rice Pablum. "Come see," she says.

It is the trailer of a country music queen, a star's dressing room. Soft corners and thick light. Opulent mobility. Frank looks beat when we come in; he doesn't get up, barely wags his white-tipped tail. His eyes are all bloodshot. I wonder if he's jealous, just pretending to sleep, alert to every nuance.

One wall is photographs and I stand there, with my hands folded in front, like it's a field trip. Mimi Brandolini comes from behind and places yet another bottle of beer in my hand. I look at her to say thank you. I look back at the display and her fingernails quietly sift through the hair left above my ear. I look to see if the Iceman saw. I melt. Somewhere in the trailer puppies yip.

"Is this Frank?" I look at a photo with a prominent blue ribbon. Mimi isn't looking at the camera in this one. She is looking down at the leash held loosely between two hands. She is wearing a pink satin shirt and white western boots with silver toes; her hair is big. She looks like a calf-roper with a moral dilemma.

"No. That's the mum. That's Pete."

"Pete?"

"Champion Bitch Centre Ice Peter Mahovlich." She moves away from me to gaze out the small, high window. "We bury her tomorrow. My dad's coming from Montreal."

REX GRANITE COMPANY, Cloud MN

The puppies have the run of the back bedroom. The dog smell is heavy camouflage. Frank follows us in. He goes over to the brood, sniffs and shoves, and lies down among their fat bodies. They are rib-cage and senses, like me. I lift one to my face, we stare, and then my nose is gnawed, sharp teeth bringing tears to my eyes. Mimi takes the dog from me and lowers it into Frank's domain.

She is taller than I am. Her breasts reach for my shoulders. Mimi kisses my nose, my eyes, runs her small puppy tongue along my bottom lip and sneaks into my mouth. Her bracelet jangles round her wrist as she pulls the T-shirt out of her hair. I am on the bed, on top of a derelict red and yellow starburst quilt; my jeans are under the dogs. Mimi Brandolini kneels above me and starts to take off her little skirt, but I stop her. I say, "Leave it on."

My brother sees me step down out of the trailer; he's looking everywhere for me. He sees Mimi at the window. "Where've you been? Who's she?"

"Dog lover."

"I don't want to know. You smell like a kennel."

I am sucked in by tough-guy undertow, dragged back to the car in his wake. "Are you mad?" I have to say this to the back of his neck as he unlocks his door.

"I couldn't find you." I barely hear it.

"Better get used to that." Maybe he laughs. In the back seat are three enormous sacks of dog food, sitting straight up like hitchhikers. "Friends of yours?"

"Science Diet. Supplies. Don't ask me."

"What's in there?"

"Balanced Nutrition for Health and Vitality."

"No shit." I try to wind down my window, but the handle just spins. I spread my fingers and press my hands flat against the glass, but it won't give. I can hardly breathe.

We are wired driving back; no radio makes it sound faster. There are things he wants to know about me, questions he wants to ask, blanks he wants to fill in before it's too late. Details. He wants a precision memory bank, photographic. I don't mind the third degree from him, I am content to participate.

The sky is pink like Mimi Brandolini's satin shirt. We pass through Auburn, like Mimi's hair.

"What's your favourite food – " he starts.

"Ice cream," I interrupt.

"Hang on. What's your favourite food, and why?"

"Ice cream. Because it doesn't hurt."

"What's your favourite music, and why?"

"Early Beatles, same reason."

I lie on my back, knees up, my head deep in his lap. I close my eyes. I feel his muscles shift and adjust every time he looks down at me. The steering wheel sounds like it's pulling giant elastic bands.

"What are your views on the Vietnam War?"

"It was just a conflict. There are worse ways to die." His stomach laughs once and bounces my head. We did this as kids, I remember, at night in my room. We took turns bouncing and laughing, whistling in the dark, trying to keep it down. We pass Bellingham.

"You awake?" he whispers.

"Are you?" I answer.

"Okay, one more question. How would you react if you were caught in a severe fire?"

"I am caught in a severe fire. I worry for the cat."

His thigh lifts my head to brake. I start to sit up, to make myself presentable, but he stops me. "Don't worry," he whispers, and puts one hand over my eyes to shade them from the runway lights at the border.

III
Elite Hotel

Elite Hotel

Happy birthday to me. I ordered a fillet and a good dry red. I said, "Rare," and saw a picture in my mind of a city steak, tall, with charcoal running to a little deep red dead centre, colourful julienned things scattered around it. My vengeful waitress brings me mill town steak, squat and fleshy purple, with a little tarpaper black around the sides. Singed. And I didn't understand I had to order the vegetables *à la carte*. This is the middle of nowhere; who does this place think it is? I told the waitress I turn thirty today but there won't be a candle in my cherry cheesecake; she thought I was bragging.

Mert looks after atmosphere. Across the room, she plays electric piano, presumes I'm here to listen and learn. Mert has a nasty game going with my waitress (FRAN Your Waitress), some sort of coded communication when FRAN motivates around the room in support knee socks. Their eyes meet, words unspoken; they know what they're doing and it concerns me.

Mert plays a perpetual medley, plowing right through intros and codas. One songs resists, surrenders, then reluctantly becomes the next song; waltzes melt into polkas like Neapolitan ice cream at room temperature. The piano whirs and clacks and strives to be strings. When she can't stop herself, Mert sings along on a tune she cherishes. Tonight she picks "The Wayward Wind."

Mert knows I'll be singing that song later, in the lounge – *Here's an old favourite guaranteed to take you back* – and wants to remind me that anything I can do, she can do better because she's got twenty years experience, blonde hair, a piano with a thousand possibilities. She was already married and pregnant and repressed when Gogi Grant made "The Wayward Wind" a household hum. She has history with it. She sings on the beat and makes it a high school march.

I'm going on a little coffee break. More music before you know it. Mean time, take care. She is so breathy I could gag.

Mert has saved some of last week's Christmas decorations, ones she believes are fine for any occasion, and with a cup of coffee (at this hour?) in one hand, she re-sticks silver stars and red bows around the back of her piano, covers up Yamaha with tinfoil snowflakes: "These work for the whole of wintertime. FRAN? No?" She is not so breathy without an SM57 mike to break her pucker. She is shrill and obtrusive; I am trying to dine. One edge of my steak is old news, the rest reminds me of when my sheltie got run over.

In an hour I will be singing in the Overlander Lounge. A big picture of me blocks half the doorway, I can see it from here. I watch me eat. That picture is five years old and already looks like someone I wouldn't drink with. Twenty pounds layered on since then and everyone figures the extra weight is a sign I'm either very happy or very sad. I alternate; everybody's right. The hotel put spangles around my picture, and staff treat me like a mobster. It is impossible to ignore that I am from a city and have come to be the centre of attention in a place this size. Mill towns hate excess, abhor privilege.

"How's that good primed rib tonight, Mert-y?" A man with a tiny wife and a big hat explodes into the dining room. What a thing to ask a piano player. But this is ritual and Mert glows in front of my table, clutching, twisting, smoothing the hands of her regulars.

"Compliments of the new season, Mr. and Mrs. Cruickshank. To you and yours." She's gone all airy again.

"Get to work up there, Mert-y. And whatever happens, *no Christmas carols!*" says the boomy Mr. C. They all laugh; the wife hits his elbow in mock outrage, mock everything.

I am too far into my fillet to send it back, even if FRAN came within hollering distance of my table, which she won't. Each bite is more chewy. I pretend something about bovine sushi and dig in while Mert rips off more of my songs: *Ev'ry night I hope and pray a dream lover will come my way.* She says she used to have a crush on Bobby Darin so I am outranked. I never liked his looks: too slimy, too old.

And Red Crow won't call tonight. He thinks he should, has the number, and knows what times are best before and after I work. But the magic vanished over Christmas; it went so far out that we're beyond a courtesy call. The end is always right on top of me before I know what's happened.

I refuse to dwell. Two arms over my head beat the bushes for FRAN's attention. She clearly takes her time. Of course there are three of us to serve now, and all at once.

"I'd like more wine, please."

"A nice little glass?"

"Another carafe, please."

"Steak okay?"

"A little under for me."

"Shoulda said. Right back with yer vino." Which isn't exactly true. Later that same day she slams it onto the corner of my table on her way to Mr. and Mrs. Regular Cruickshank. She leans against their table like a hooker in her heyday, certain she has earned the right to slouch.

Snow on last week's Christmas Eve afternoon, half an hour into the drive from here south to Red Crow, I can't see broad daylight beyond the steering wheel. Austin Marina, fish out of water. A long stretch beside where the lake always was till now, changing altitude filling my head with explosives. The voice of my first boyfriend the only other time I drove in snow: "Pretend it's the Indy 500. You're Mario Andretti." I want to pull over to panic but there's no way to tell what's road and what's lake. The radio's gone. Monte Lake, the sign small and reflecting all that white glare like high beams. Why would they name a lake after my mother's hairdresser? We're all going too fast to be a traffic jam. It's so quiet. *Too quiet*, ha. I swerve to miss a small giant boulder in my path, though I'm not exactly sure where my path is. I've never been able to judge where these wheels touch down or what my clearance is on either side. Spatial problems; on thin ice. I swerve but hit it and it's just a clump of oily snow, but I'm sideways in the other lane, the inevitable demon semi upon me. The man inside it is pulling on his horn, as if that'll help. He is a professional driver, I'm a singer. I could've spent Christmas in my hotel room and avoided all this peril. When will I learn to stay put.

Back on my own side; I didn't even lose my place in this phantom convoy, that's how fast it was. I'm over the hump. My ears pop; decrescendo. The sky is clear, 97 is bare and dry. This way to the sunny Okanagan. What was that all about? Radio's back, some old blues guy predates Elvis, *bay-aybee tryin' to get to you.*

I went through Red Crow's drawers and closets last summer. He went to the bar for more prefab beer; the homemade stuff was guzzled and gulped the morning I got there. While he was gone, I, wearing his cleanest dirty T-shirt, scouted the area for vice. You look for it, you find it. Shoved back in the bedroom closet, bunched up and off-colour, classic examples of stripper get-up. Dusty sequins sewn on netting with the wrong colour thread. Too opaque. The black velvet half-bra enormous and wired. Discards or souvenirs or house system.

Imagine the two of them in private performance. She cranks up mid-tempo blues on the stereo, boosts the bass while he makes himself comfortable with home-brew and mildewed feather pillows across the mattress on the floor. They have piled dirty jeans and damp towels into a darkening corner. They have permanently repositioned a stereo speaker for these regular occasions. This is how they always do it; she's that creative. Her hair smells clean. Pink curtains are drawn shut and persistent twilight does things to the walls. She is so confident I can't go through with it.

"How come you ate it if it was so bad?" FRAN disappears through a swinging door. One door is still pumping open-and-shut when FRAN shoves through the other one, carrying my cheesecake like a drawn pistol.

"Enjoy," she cautions, reaching over to the next table for the fork. I hate it when they bring the dessert and I have half the wine to go. The cheesecake is wrinkled and cracked on top, like butterscotch pudding. No whipped cream, no cherries, no candle, No Exit, no rest for the weary.

Friday night in April and I was playing his bar, trying to rock it up for people who need a band in order to think straight. I shuffled through kindergarten Chuck Berry licks but they didn't buy it. The population of his town is low four figures, and most wandered through on that night. Red Crow brought a brandy up to the stage on his way out, did that thing with his cowboy hat, the one you see the guys on *Bonanza* do when there's a woman (at last) around: "Ma'am."

Word got out or spread like wildfire that I wasn't danceable and the next night the bar was all but empty; the owner sat at a far-off table sulking over figures, rubbing it in. Then Red Crow came in with enough friends and extended family to take up the best tables. They danced, they sang along, they drank pitchers of beer with pricey chasers; no one got punched. Sometimes they remembered to clap. I was welcome in their midst on my breaks; Red Crow saved me a padded chair, one with arms. Every time he got up to use the can, he touched my shoulder lightly with his fist. Once, he did it on his way back, as he sat down; no eye contact, just that. At the end of the night, feeling star struck by my own presence, I decided on yes or no to his inevitable proposition. I am an expert. With experience, I have learned to drink just enough beer over an evening to justify either answer, to back up either choice.

"Some of us are heading up to the homestead in the morning. I'll be out front at nine if you're coming. You should. You'll like it up there on the mountain. Get you out of the bars, into air."

He smiled and chewed a corner of his mustache, did the Little Joe routine with his hat again, and made his back straight for the walk out the open doors of his bar. The long, half-breed black braid made him look like my best friend Sari from grade three. An omen of some kind: we were only best friends for one grade, then she left me for a taller girl with blonde hair and lots of shoes.

"Mind if I sit? This way I don't have to go and sit with Cruickshanks and listen to *the Unions* this and *the Unions* that. You know what I'm talking about, you see it in this business. Gee, that piano's pretty from here."

This feels like work. Like taking a break and finding out every lonely person in the room has been waiting to buy you a drink and ask, "So, are you on some kind of circuit?" Mert's arm languishes across my table. The nerve of a permanent fixture. "Like to share my wine?" I offer, remembering my manners.

"Are you kidding? One sip and I'm all thumbs and fingernails. My late husband warned me never to mix business with libation. He was right, as usual. About me, at least. I lose track and I don't think that honours the music. These songs we're doing deserve every bit of care and attention we can give them. We have a gift, and gifts are for giving. Every night. It not only pays the bills but it brightens my back yard, my little bit of paradise. So how was the steak?"

"A little under for me."

"That's unusual. In the eight years I've been playing that piano –"

"Giving."

"That's it. In all this time I've never seen a steak go back through those doors. Sid's the best chef this town's got. Bar none. We're lucky."

Mrs. Cruickshank has a clean paper napkin up to her mouth and some sort of horror in her eyes; tears holed up. She's looking furtively at each empty table, as though eavesdroppers are paying attention. When she takes her hands down, her lipstick has gone missing; her mouth is changing shape like an amoeba in a petri dish.

"How could you even suggest this to me, Russell?" The words make it out and through the room.

"I'm not saying we absolutely *need* to, I'm not carving it in stone. I just said we might want to give it some thought. For later, maybe. Here's the meal."

FRAN places a hand on Mr. C's shoulder and says softly, to his ear, "You watch that plate. Hot-hot."

"Mind a suggestion?" Now Mert has both arms across my table and I feel the taut wires of rank being pulled again.

"I don't know, Mert. Does it have to be tonight?"

"It just seems to me, from what I've seen of your little show — "

"I don't do a show. I sing. I use a Strat, I use a beat box with real drum sounds. That's not a show."

"What I'm saying — try not to get so defensive about what I'm just trying to explain. Talk to the people, is all. Just talk to your audience. Let them see you care about them as human beings. Ask them questions, tell them stories, funny ones about people just like them, or maybe something embarrassing that's happened to you. They want to get to know you, to sympathize. If they don't care, they won't be back tomorrow night. They definitely will find something else to do Friday and Saturday night, so, there, you've lost your weekend crowd. And maybe then you won't be back either."

I lift my fork to make it clear I intend to start in on the cheesecake. I have finished the wine, picking up the empty glass several times to make sure I got it all. "I'm a singer, not a hooker. The songs are it."

Mert raps the table gently with both hands at once. She seems to think she's done her best, that the problem is now, more than ever, mine. "I'll just start off with some nice western. For you." The last four words go breathy. She thinks I'm an invalid.

Mert starts off with a sleepy, instrumental "Help Me Make It Through the Night." Though there is no dance floor, Mr. C has yanked his wife into his enormous green-chain arms. They zoooom around the room, the skirt of her knee-length cocktail dress occasionally twirling, her slip showing, her black patent slingbacks skimming the carpet. Mert can't help it. When she gets to the bridge, she belts it out, too high, too much oxygen. Mr. C's eyes flutter open to wink at me or FRAN or Mert. He spins his wife for effect. His hat never leaves his head.

No one has offered me coffee and the dessert is over. Here comes FRAN, tallying my bill to a synchronous thirty dollars, licking the end of her pencil to cover inflation. Mert seems to have forgotten the verse about yesterday being dead and gone.

It was raining at eight-thirty, but I did it anyway. I loaded my speakers into the trunk, camouflaged the rest of the gear under a blanket on the back seat, found the bar owner, got paid, didn't get asked back. By eight-forty-five I was out front, willing to give Red Crow till five past nine and no more. He drove up as I fine-tuned my ultimatum.

A generic 4X4. Fenders and flanks riddled with pockmarks and major dings, other people's paint. Big tires all around. Red Crow parked in the middle of the street, rolled his window down; it would only go so far. His hair hung loose under the cowboy hat; he was trying to eat a green apple and smile at me at the same time. Other vehicles pulled up behind him and idled roughly. I had to shout over Main Street, Sunday morning coming down.

"Should I follow you?"

Red Crow laughed and lobbed the apple core at the jeep thing behind him. "You'd never make it. Lock it up and climb in."

Stepping up into the seat reminded me of getting on a horse, minus the leather creaks and smell. I tried for cowgirl cool, spreading my fingers over my thighs, tucking in my chin and eyebrows for a serious look through the cracked windshield, up at the drab sky. Seat belts are for cities.

"You'll want to wear this. Otherwise your head goes through the roof and I'm under-insured." He dug out one half of the seat belt and placed it across the top of my thigh.

Say goodbye to riparian zones I have known. It's early for me. I get quiet and watch for critters in the bushes as we climb and climb, switchback and climb. My head almost hits the roof. Terrain I don't recognize, complicated trees. I could use a beer.

It takes ninety minutes, straight up, to reach this place, but right off it's worth it. The rain forgets about making my morning moody. What I didn't get is that no one lives in the log house any more. Red Crow et al. figure it was built by a husband and farm wife team at the turn of the century. But no one's lived in it since any of them can remember. It is two abandoned stories, doors and windows now just clean space; outbuildings stand crooked in the field. Freelance cows have wandered into no-man's-land; they give us the eye.

Our group has seen the house a million times, so Red Crow takes me over and in while they unload supplies. There were outside stairs to the second floor at one time, but their disintegration doesn't stop us. He grabs my waist from behind and lifts me straight up. My breasts heave; I am Fay Wray. I scramble and wrench and lift my knees askew but manage to crawl in. He waits below.

Barn swallows dipping, swirling inside, panicked and amused by my intrusion. How many children did this couple squeeze into how many beds up here? I wonder about the rules, the hours, the jokes so far from town. The upstairs is already stuffy at this hour, in this weather. What was there to bicker over without the twentieth century?

There is a way downstairs. Vertical ladders make me freeze, but I get down, backwards, and Red Crow is at the window watching cows.

"Got your wallpaper picked out?" He's chewing jerky now, smiling again. Bright blue eyes in this light. Black hair/blue eyes: my father warned of these.

"Well, I'll move in tomorrow but there'll be a problem when I plug in my amp. And the agents will have a bitch of a time getting through. That could be the bonus. Otherwise, it's me." This floor is one room, too small for anything but basics: simple pleasures, cast iron, bird nests. I like the sound my shoes make on the wood floor, our voices make off the kitchen walls. Where'd everybody sit at night?

He offers me the jerky. "Last year's," he says. "Moose."

A campfire, Red Crow's friends, two brothers, a sister and her three kids, one an infant bundled, rocked, and nursed. It's still damp and cool from the rain. We eat mule deer sausage on sticks and drink Red Crow's beer and his sister's berry wine. One of the brothers takes a beer out to the field but turns back when the bull's front legs move apart and the bull's head droops to get a better look. Early Elvis, during intros.

They ask questions about my work, their faces round and eyes sincere; communally concerned about my well-being. They are not fascinated but saddened by the news of how my living makes me. They don't ask about music, except the sister says, "I don't think our bar is the right place for you, but you sure have a pretty voice. I liked every song." Her kids throw rocks at distant sacred cows, lose their balance following through.

"You still here?"

"I'd like a brandy. Heated." She makes a flourish picking up my bill for this annoying revision. She stays at my side to do the crossing out and inserting and her mouth moves, sputters, backtracks through arithmetic.

She mumbles, "Must be nice to have that kind of job." Off she goes. Back she comes. It's warm, but just. I toast the poster of me across the lobby and promise to cut down this year. My thirties will do wonders.

This letter was what tracked me down in November and led me to believe in Christmas: ". . . and I think of you pedastalled amongst The City's furtive finest and my knuckles turn white like issolated blizzards. My heart goes out to you but its hardly a substitute for a heartbeat in the darkness beside you. Long nights, spin your magic, play your music. This is my song, its the onely one I ever wrote that I remembered. You have a proud mans love. Red Crow."

I was supposed to bring enough wine for three days, but the Monte Lake 500 left me sure I'd get stuck if I stopped anywhere. Every parking lot had leftover snow. When I got to Red Crow's around seven Christmas Eve, the house was unlocked and lonely. House, hardly. A white box originally meant to sleep a migrant orchard worker or two.

On the wall above the phone is a calendar depicting winter as seen by a woman's big healthy breasts. She is in a golf cart, holding a club – a driver – wearing only earmuffs and ski boots and smiling wholeheartedly. I flip through the other months, and they are all golfing/breast scenes. One is a golfing/bending over to tee up scene. He golfs?

On top of the stereo speaker is a picture of me at the homestead, looking giddy and plump, a mug of what was berry wine extended to the cows in a toast to I don't remember what. Next to that is a professionally rendered shot of a little blonde girl wearing a pink turtleneck. I'm bad with kids, but I'd say five years old. She is shy. Around her neck is a leather thong and from it hangs a battered eagle feather, down past the middle of her chest. Her shoulders lean forward; her body is concave.

He's been listening to vintage Emmylou Harris, so I know he's been thinking about me, boning up on what it takes. I put on the same side he was listening to and try to mind my own business.

Someone's acting like a family, coming through the back door into the kitchen. Red Crow wears clean jeans and an ironed shirt with the cuffs done up. It looks brand new. The little girl has on a red and white velvet dress, also an aura of brand new, maybe a special gift from Dad though I don't know how he made his cheque go that far. She has red patent-leather shoes and a crinoline. The woman is smoking and undoing the zipper on her white satin jeans: "Me First Me First. Outta my way." She topples past me in silver stilettos.

Red Crow sparks like he's been drinking rye. He puts his fist on the girl's shoulder and says. "Go get the brush. It's in the bedroom."

"*Mom,*" she shouts at the bathroom door, "*I get to do Dad's hair.*"

"Hurry up we gotta go."

He finally says hello to me, kisses my cheek. Puts his hand along the side of my face. Smells of rye, sure enough. Emmylou goes: *Seems like this whole town's insane.* He sits cross-legged on the floor, brings his braid up front and pulls the elastic off.

"That's my job," the girl whines, waving the brush at him. She sounds tired, pushed too far, up too late.

"Get to work, then."

She separates the three sections of hair by sticking a small finger in each little braid hole and pulling down with expert strokes.

"Hurry up I said. Hi, I'm Shyanne call me Anne. Take the fuckin' elastic outta your mouth it's been in your dad's hair. For Christ Almighty you shouldna give it to her Bob. Where's your brain. Sorry, too much wine, I get loud."

The girl gets in maybe a dozen tender strokes through Red Crow's hair, down his back, before the mother grabs the girl's arm and throws the brush onto the couch beside me. "You finish up, honey." The girl is sobbing and trying not to leave, digging her heels into plywood and rag rugs. She gets hauled away. Red Crow hasn't moved.

"Very festive," I say.
"Did you bring wine?"
"Nope. Sorry."
"Then it won't be. There's nothing here and town's shut down. You said you'd bring it."
"I couldn't get to the store. The snow was sticking. So why no mention of a kid?"

He shouts all but the first word. "Because. That would be a lie because there's another one in Thunder Bay. Because it was none of your business. Because I didn't want to. I don't need reasons here. This is my life here." He goes to the bedroom and slams the door so the windows rattle and the record skips to the end. I saddle up, wondering why he didn't just break something or hit me. Where will the snow kick in on my way back; what about black ice in the dark?

Twenty minutes before work. FRAN has been paid and over-tipped due to some stupid act of solidarity on my part. She sees the Cruickshanks out; Mert waves at them from the kitchen door. She's done for the night. "Showtime!" she says to me.

I follow out into subzero, multiple feet of snow; no coat. I want to see my car. There it is, way off across the parking lot at the worst table in the house. It's impossible to tell the colour with all the snow on it, around it, climbing the tires. I left the driver's door unlocked so it wouldn't freeze; it still takes muscle to open but I can do it. The seats won't give. The light inside is dim, indirect, arctic. I am an Inuit, a weary bear performing hibernation, I am into cryonics.

All I have in the pocket of my jeans is a key to Room 202. My car keys are there, on top of the television. Forget it. Once I'm upstairs I will no longer have what I have at this moment down here, behind the wheel: a feel for locomotion.

    The snow scares me. I need to get paid before I can buy gas.

    FRAN and Mert block the entrance, arms around waists, kicking their feet like freezing, aged Rockettes. They sing *Let it snow Let it snow Let it snow* in unison, though FRAN doesn't quite make all the words. They pull apart to usher me through, feet still kicking, arms now waving lazily above their heads. Off-shift dizzy. Mert adds a little simple harmony.

    Ten minutes and I still have to tune up.

Magnetic Creeping

At the gas station in the city, the teenage boy leering in at Dixie's bare thighs swimming in the bucket seat. With an oily finger, he pretended to trace the slice of cracked windshield; he lingered, and rubbed too long at fly shit. She pulled her skirt down. Jim watched her do it, caught the boy watch her do it. And on the overloaded car ferry, when the little girl in coveralls stopped to stare at Dixie's stump, the place where the long-gone left hand should be, and said – just between them – "Did it hurt?"

Dixie will remember the boy's ponytail and his resemblance to every other cold and dark teenager on the planet; Jim will remind her about his name tag: Newt. She might discuss the girl on the ferry in terms of how different children are from adults, how they are openhearted and explicit and we, as adults, are doomed by a need to modify behaviour, to smooth off edges and watch our tongues. Jim will remember that the little girl stopped on her way down the aisle to look back at him fiercely, as if he had something to do with Dixie's missing hand. He left Dixie on Promenade Deck, took the stairs to the car, to be below sea level. Seagulls and spindrift sailed backwards past the car.

Gran and Alfred have not met Dixie, but Jim has spared no expense doling out details so there will be no surprises. The first phone call to Gran, the one to say "we're coming" ended with:

"Don't expect a woman with one hand to dry dishes, Gran. Give it some thought before we get there." Jim's grandmother wanted to know if Dixie would be wearing a plastic hand or would they get to see the smooth nub of her arm. The second phone call, the one to confirm plans, ended this way: "Don't expect Dixie to be interested in which of your friends has cataracts, or who said what to the Chinese minister at St. Mary's. She's a little on the smart side, Gran. She's gone to school in France." Gran wanted to know if Dixie likes rhubarb and if she would be willing to have a look at some old life insurance policies to "see about the money."

"Does she like to sing, Jimmy?" she wanted to know.

He called Gran this morning, before leaving. At the end of the call, he reminded her that Dixie is special, not a bit like the others. "Are you coming through downtown, Jimmy, or will you take the new overpass?" was all she wanted to know.

In front of the house on Princess Street – clean lines, a porch, early summer heat sparkling off old stucco, running into the eaves – Jim almost parks the car at the curb but remembers Alfred objects: the street is too narrow and other drivers warrant clear passage from one end of the block to the other; he does his bit. So they take the driveway and pull up close to the garage door. Inside is a mauve 1968 Impala with crackling plastic covers on the seats. A car that has never been over a speed limit, has had double the requisite oil changes, needs the battery terminals scraped and the water topped up. On the back wall of the garage is a wooden sign, a plank: BC ELECTRIC. Jim's real grandfather was a lineman. Each summer, after hydro came, his grandparents visited a different dam and sent photos of Gramps pointing out a travelogue sheet of water, smiling as if he paved its way, thought the whole thing up. The sign is not cheap reminiscence on Gran's part. It is a cenotaph.

Up in the rafters, French doors are piled three deep, two across. Bug webs cover cracked glass, the wood bends and buckles and paint peels back. They've rested there since Jim was old enough to look up and notice. Gran had them taken out of the house twenty years ago, trying to achieve The Open Plan Look.

"Your grandmother's looking at me out the window. Don't kiss me, she'll get the wrong idea. I should've worn pants. Don't put your arm around me all the time; I don't want her to think it's just sex. And *don't* tell her how my husband died." Long walk off a short pier under the influence of every drug in the book. She dared him, head first into water deep enough to cover only a fraction of his bloated body. Jim was the do-good buddy who hauled him out with the ridiculous thought, "I can't let him drown," his own knee wrenched and wrecked on driftwood, a ligament severed in an act of guilty heroism. The night before, Dixie and her husband doing soft things in the next room, Jim had the thought: "If he was dead she'd want me."

Gran is in the rear-view mirror, pulsing up the driveway like a novice hiker. Her arms hold each other in for aerodynamics, a pale blue cardigan hangs over her tiny shoulders: maple leaf sweater guard, as always. She raps her wedding rings on the back window, then the one on Dixie's side; she clatters them on the window right beside Dixie's face. They wave to each other, fingers trying to meet and make acquaintance. Gran points at the lock on the door. Dixie reaches, lifts it, removes her seatbelt, one-handed. Dixie's missing hand is an elegy to the smack she did at her husband's wake, a sustained and lonely tie-off that made her fingers go blue then black. They all allowed her to grieve, until she screamed for them to stop.

The door is open and the women lurch and embrace. "Everything is still warm," Gran says as the two women walk up the drive and past the garage, almost out of sight. They are entwined. "I hope you like rhubarb." Dixie's purse is still on the back seat. Jim picks it up and wears it like she does, the strap diagonal on his chest, the way a cowboy packs a canteen.

Across the backyard lawn, Alfred emerges from the raspberry patch in time to escort Jim up the back steps. He is tall and straight – his own clean lines. This is Gran's second husband, replacing a real grandfather Jim remembers only in terms of hands and huge thumbs, who died of something cerebral. Water, maybe. Alfred will always sound like a traitor to Jim's loyal ears.

Alfred shakes Jim's hand, supports his elbow. He looks at the purse and doesn't get it but moves on. "Have you *ever* seen a clematis so glorious, Jim-boy?" He turns Jim to look back at the garage. A Rubens Montana covers the entire side with a thick mat of rosy-pink and purple star blooms. Jim gave it to Gran ten years ago, a six-inch shoot off one of his own, told her where to plant it. It has taken an Oriental turn, an aesthetic bend around door jamb and broken window.

"There must be something keeping the root system cool," Jim says slowly, taking credit.

"Bullshit," Alfred shouts. "Lots of it."

The kitchen is hard white. Dixie and Gran are already sipping sherry in the breakfast nook. All hands reach and point, flat out. There is no deception at this table. The beige carpet makes everything sound flat and pleasant, venetian blinds stripe faces, pale arms; conversation threads. A perfectly round electric Westclox whirs gently on the wall behind Gran's head. In another ten years, that clock will be from another era, a collectible, post-war, pre-destiny. Alfred brings in a beer, poured too high into a glass with a picture of Hoover Dam on it. There is a thin line of foam, the beer too warm to frost the glass.

"Alfred. This is Jimmy's friend. Dixie, my second husband,

Alfred. No need to shake her hand, Alfred. She's drinking sherry just now."

Alfred looks at Jim. Dixie puts down the tiny glass and holds out her hand to Alfred. He beams; he kisses it and hides it in both of his for a moment.

Gran won't allow sports on Sunday, no games at all, so there is Sunday afternoon nature show music from the television in the den. As on all of Jim's childhood weekends, a calm man says:

> *The impala remains close to dense trees and bushes with easy access to water, and when alarmed it can leap up to thirty-five feet to disappear into the nearest cover. Large herds form in winter, but in summer they travel in smaller family groups.*

"Come on downstairs, Jim-boy. I'll show you something. Let these gals alone."

The basement is a half-light shrine to Jim's real grandfather. Alfred has left everything pretty much the way Gramps had it. The air is subterranean and smells of dry cedar and algae.

The workbench is fraught with sockets and plugs and wires coming and going. An electric kettle shaped like a collector's item has no cord, though an ancient one, wrapped with red and black striped cloth, droops over a cardboard wastebasket. A dormant, curvy toaster. It is hard to breathe. This is the real grandfather's midden.

"We had to disconnect the old telephone. Your grandfather had it hooked up out-of-wedlock, so to speak, and I don't want any part of that. I was hearing something unlawful coming over the radio, too, so I put that away. The one with all the little tubes. I'd like to see what I can get for that old GE. Early twenties, semi-high oven, deep-well cooker. An old Hotpoint. It's a beauty, but we don't entertain enough to use it." The white enamel is flawless. The stove's tiny clock, stranded behind greasy glass, shows the correct time.

Above the cleft telephone is a mint-condition calendar: August 1967. Snap-On Tools. The woman in the picture sits demurely by current standards, but the tops of her big breasts show, meeting in the middle and pushing out of a polka-dot bathing suit. Her skin is white, fleshy, unmarked, and untanned. There are no muscles anywhere. She hides her hands behind her back; her breasts respond, shoulders rounded and caught back. And her mouth. Open lips, white teeth through red, tongue touching the two in front. As a boy, alone down here on no-sports Sundays, Jim stared and kept one hand inside the waistband of his pants. Blue eyes and black hair; standards of beauty and arousal came from this picture. "A girl like that," he promised himself, checked other months, but always came back to this one.

"Roy Patterson used to be a rep for Snap-On. I think your grandfather hung that up just to please old Roy. He was embarrassed by that kind of thing."

The television drones above us. Gran's heels click across dated linoleum. Small steps, hurrying to make a point, or tea.

"Come into the other side," says Alfred. "Have a look at *my* little corner of the world.

"Wait." There is a photograph, thumb-tacked above the laundry tub, of Jim's real grandfather, posing in front of a mystery dam. He is proud of something, and angry, too. "Where was this taken?"

"Oh. Ha. Bone of contention. That's the Hart Dam, over on the Island, just south of where you are. I knew your grandfather for forty years, and we had our first and only almost-come-to-blows over it. Too many people lost too much over that dam, I thought. A bunch of us from the juice gang could see plain as day what it was gonna do to the land around there. Screw it up for good, pardon the French. We spoke our minds about it.

"Your grandfather thought I was nuts. More than that. He thought I was crossing over to the other side. Took it personally. He had a whole stack of those pictures made up. Sent me one a week for the longest time. No note, just that picture, looking like he owns the place."

Jim tries a simple chord but it sounds too complicated. The piano is still out of tune by a mile. Through the window above it, the front tires of the car and Dixie's legs. Only her calves scoot by. He leans up and knocks with one knuckle, but she must not know where the sound is coming from. Her feet are bare.

"Here you go, Jim-boy. This is what your Gran calls 'Alfred's Contribution To The Power Bill.'"

It is a maybe fifty-gallon fish tank, a cistern, laid out on top of the grandparents' antique wedding table, the oak one Gran says they bought at auction on their wedding day. Back lit. Snails rush to clear the glass.

"I'm still figuring things out. I had a gourami in there for a while but the guppies lost their tails and all their babies disappeared. So I flushed that one. Now it's just the tetras, a few guppies, and the Chinese algae eater. But I'll get more. Something orange."

The real grandfather's collection of glass insulators are nestled into the white sand. Mauve and blue domes like aboriginal dwellings. Artifacts. "When I was a boy," says Alfred, "we used to throw rocks at those things to try and break 'em. Then Hydro went to ceramic and it couldn't be done." The school shifts a fraction of a degree and flashes neon. An amber light comes on in the water; the whole basement reacts, dims, regains its strength.

They are singing. Dixie is damp and laughing and washing dishes, up to one elbow in barely sudsy water. The dishrack has been moved over to the right side of the sink to accommodate her handicap. Gran flaps a dish towel, waiting for the next bowl. *If it takes forever, I will wait for you. For a thousand summers, I will wait for you.* Alfred joins in. He holds Gran by the waist and they serenade the moment between them, Gran's hands under the towel, clasped discreetly at her heart. Dixie is flushed on one side of her face; her bare legs are crossed at the ankles to make one thick stem. She knows all the words.

Two possibilities: mating for life might be a strategy to promote successful evolution, or it could ensure species extinction if one mate dies and the other is unable to move on. There are two men missing from this room, only Jim seems to remember that. He feels the urge to save a life. He has to leave the room.

The man in the den remains calm but his French accent sounds thicker:

> *The finback whale is gracefully streamlined and a very fast swimmer, dark-coloured with white underparts; the head markings are asymmetrical.*

The attic is warm and close and sweet. They lie under a pale blue sheet. Gran has placed white freesia and alyssum in crystal on the night table. One small, open window looks next door. Antique lace limits moonlight.

His head on the feather pillow, Jim imagines walking on the ceiling, the weight of dead men off his shoulders. Dixie whispers, "I'm glad you brought me." She kisses his bad knee, her hand cupped supportively behind it. "I've found you here, I think." She breathes hard at his hip. A curtain moves. "And here." Almost erect in the house of his real grandfather. Her blue eyes between his legs, Dixie is a mile downstream, setting stakes; a weir. It is the single bed of his youth, but tonight there is lots of room.

He pulls on her arm; licks the stump, places it over his eye, and over the other one. She is above, her legs long over his: twenty toes.

Grief Work

At two a.m. I wandered downstairs and found Richard draping himself over the kitchen table, his arms stretched out, trying to prevent levitation. Richard likes for things to remain firmly fixed. On the ground. But he can't hold down his mother, who has been drifting up and away for several weeks, tangled and lashed by twelve-pound test to a husband who keeps her motivated and a son who sulks. She's trying to die as fast as she can, but no one is quick to cut her loose. They won't even let her go to the hospital for fear she will disappear in there. Richard hugs Vilas maple, bound by tradition.

I tried bashing my way out of the dark. "What the fuck are you doing up?" I said this, believe it or not.

"Thinking. Writing."

I stood in the doorway, my hands on my hips, wearing my red kimono inside out. A belligerent toreador looking for a bull in a china shop. "You're doing what? You're *writing*? You're doing a little *writing* are you? Well." I circled the table. "Aren't you the literate one Aren't you somebody's idea of the ultimate man What a *man* you are You and your fucking fountain pen down here in the dark writing macho puke. What do you think you're doing? Papa-fucking-Hemingway."

"'It's really not anything. It's just to let the air in.'"

My hands came away from my hips. The belt fell off my robe. Richard was sitting up and I could see his journal and the pen; he had been sprawled on top of them. An almost empty carafe, a full glass of burgundy. Richard gazing out into side street, hands folded on his lap, looking like a student whose attention has wandered. Teachers call those boys daydreamers.

"Richard," I said firmly, standing across from him.

He turned to me and said, "Would you please please please please please please please stop talking."

I flipped the wine out of the glass, into his eyes, his hair, down his neck; some stained the white wall behind his head and my bare stomach; most ended up in his journal. I went back up to bed. Later, I heard him down there sobbing, but I thought I'd only make the whole thing worse by showing up.

I got up at four this morning.

The pilot wears jewellery. There is a rope of orange gold at his throat and a matching one on his wrist. I offer my hand across deserted blacktop like this is a first date or a political intrigue. His rings hurt my knuckles; he squeezes too hard and I'm sure he knows it; why do they do that? His belt buckle is an icon, a face etched into imitation brass but I can't look down because he'll think . . . it's a cowboy, or Beethoven.

It is so early and clear this feels like a camping trip, my first date with Richard, he afraid the hatchet would need sharpening and checking under the hood for omens, me afraid of cystitis in the woods with no sulfa. But the sky was chlorinated blue and there was more air than we deserved. The chill meant it was an act of zeal. Crack of dawn shows everything. Like today.

"Careful on those steps" means he is looking up at my legs in these shoes and this skirt. The sound of his voice winds around my ankles; hog-tied, I may fall and roll into the plane, my skirt will hike past the tide lines on my pantyhose, he'll see white cotton frozen stiff under beige beige beige unsanitary unsexy. "Isn't there an alternative to those things? Can't we compromise on this?" My husband Richard, our second date.

A young woman buries her summer thighs in paperwork; she has the window. White shoes and bare shoulders at this hour: teenage. Her face scarred. No, just the cheek and some pockmarks around the ear. I hope it will some day be treated and healed. Not so men will honour her; I just want there to be one less worry. When she looks in the mirror at thirty-five, I want her to have one less obsession. "Would it be okay if *you* sat by the window and I sat *there*? It's going to be my first time," she says. She is already up and shifting belongings and making sure her short skirt has not drifted too high in the back. It has; I smell this morning and her boyfriend, or it could be last night and a stranger, but it's there at my face, like Old Dutch Cleanser and deodorant soap that didn't get it all. She *must* be afraid if she'll give up the window.

"Once we're off the ground, you'll forget. I fly a lot and here I am." I am authority.

"Did you know you had a run all the way up your leg?" She is a smoker obeying signs. I know by the way her mouth twitches. Like Richard's mother's. Lips that would rather squeeze something than let go of a word, a breath. Cigarettes help to measure pulse beat, hand shake. Time. "Buckle up, ladies." The pilot is a new man with equipment around his head, at his controls. In the cockpit. But maybe I'm making too much of this.

We taxi – is it called that in a plane this small? Cessna 150, 180, 1-something. This is the closest I come to out-of-body. The pressure, the scream inside, out. And all the air shifting and circulating and taking part in the act of elevation, an active part in buoyancy. Air invisible and huge, pulling itself through twin engines (maybe it's a Beaver) and lifting the tail and cushioning wings. Still in here. I want to open the window and get some support.

But we are airborne. The young woman is looking all over her face with her fingertips – a reconnaissance – scouting sites for more mutilation. The curls on this side of her head are flat from sleep. Tapered nails occasionally poke at them, try to achieve symmetry for anyone who should look at her straight on, from the front. This is habit. She makes me want to fidget. I assume this is a return flight for her, a shuttle back to the Sunshine Coast after visiting her boyfriend (a stranger?) in Big City. Her shoes, so white and such stiff leather, lead me to believe she is out of her element. And she has too much skin exposed to be from an International Airport town. Long flawless arms, long legs conspicuously hair-free. But she said "first time."

"Are you going home for the weekend?" She asks me. The pilot says something overseas; not a foreign language, but he's too far away to understand. They could spring for new speakers at these rates.

"I'm going up on business." I am the perfect example. Suited and low-heeled in navy, I am coordinated. My hair is an every-two-months, look-the-same-as-always cut; it falls into place. One diamond ring. One silk scarf. A satchel, not a (too manly) briefcase.

Look at me; you could do this.

"I have to go to court," she says proudly, older. "This hotel owner? He hired me for two weeks – I've got the contract – then he dumps me after one. The bar's dead so he blames me and shit I just got there. The chick they had the week before me? I asked around and some agent out of *Abbotsford* sent her. Called herself *Chrysler*. She should of used a wheelchair. So business is the shits, they say it's me, and I get canned. I *drove* all the way there, I had to take *two* ferries, and they didn't even pay for it. What do *you* do?"

"I sell Business Communications Systems." I bore her. "Telephones," I embellish.

Ground Support Equipment, and it's transporting one suitcase, mine. All the way in from our little plane to the terminal where the young woman waits with me to share a cab to town, my tan leather suitcase sits in the middle of some guy's union job; he's a speed demon in a cartoon.

"It looks lonely," she says. She fell asleep on my shoulder, missed touchdown, and is now a sad girl. Not because something was missed; this is her regular morning mood, she says. It's before eight, she'll recover and get on with it. I have an appointment to go over a System with the owner of the hotel she is suing.

"Just watch out for that guy," she says and puts a fingernail in her mouth. So sad.

Our cab driver is treated to the story about getting fired and going to court. The girl is in the front seat. He remembers this story and tells how he heard it, sympathizes. Although he says we are the first fare today, he smells of personal rot. "About how much you gals make a week give or take don't mind me asking?" She can't say. I don't know if he means me. "Tips any good?" He is performing an indecent act of forcible communion.

"Depends what you mean by tip." She is all of a sudden sultry.

She is slow to contribute her half of the fare, but I don't offer to cover the whole thing even though it's a write-off for me. I figure she has bargaining power with the driver; they are awfully chummy after fifteen minutes, she can tip. She isn't so sad any more. I walk away from the car with long adult strides. "Take care now," she calls to me, but I've heard this bullshit before. Too friendly, too early, too soon; putting on an act for the man.

It is called The Inn at Westview, but my room faces east. I will spend the day and night and catch what will probably be the plane I just got off first thing tomorrow. A full circle if I want to cram some meaning into all this. My circuit covers every profitable business in this town, anything the Receiver General won't be picking over next month. I don't sell, just introduce concepts, but it's important not to piss anyone off, especially the women. I used to be a "Communications Hostess," but some survey showed how that made people think "apron." Now they call me "rep"; I think German shepherd.

The sun sets in the east, through cheap Day-Glo curtains, across the bed. You have to walk too much in ship route towns. I walked from one end of the water street to the other; everyone knows they don't know you. Service is slow, making some point about colonization: "Don't even think about it." And then I walked up that impossible hill to avoid the smell of another cab driver, bought good red wine on the way. Half a glass put me to sleep, fully clothed.

The phone rang to stop a dream about cowboys. Two good guys holed up in a gulch by two bad guys. It was a movie. One of the good guys was an Indian, I could tell by the way he stood straight, looked calm no matter what. The bad guys took naps on a plaid couch right there in the gulch. They had their way with a little boy who had a choirboy mouth. He wore two wigs. Like Richard's mother.

"She's gone, sweetheart," Richard dripping pathos into the phone.

"When will she be back? Where'd they take her this time?"

Part of me is trying to head this news off at the pass. I want to hang up.

"Can you come back tonight? I checked, there's a flight. I could use some help with this. Dad's rough."

"Ruff," I bark back. Rin Tin Tin makes an entrance – show off – and rescues cavalry men in pale blue. Someone's knotted a red bandanna around his neck. He looks too detailed. I don't know what happened to Richard. All I know is, there's a set sun out there and someone knocking at This Room at The Inn.

"Sorry. Would you have a hair dryer I can borrow?" His chest is miraculously hairy. I rap my inner knuckles for lusting over a barefoot-chest-arms Marlboro Man; I am a product of something. Blue jeans, one white rip. Who wouldn't. I'd be sick if I just said no way I'm allowed to look at that, did it, and lied about it. That's a problem with sex. And I don't. Lie, have a problem.

"It's not exactly high-tech, but it blows." I can't believe the things that slither out of this mouth. Now I can't look; I just close the door on his thanks. And I wonder why people find me hard.

I leave the lights off and lie down; now, where was I. A full water glass of wine. The TV is on next door, my head is inches from the wall that separates us. It is a comedy with a laugh track for aesthetic guidance, and every time the TV people laugh, a real man laughs too. He booms, surrounded by loved ones. Theme music I can't place – synthesized – and a commercial for . . .

The sound of my hairdryer. And low laughing now that is intimate and caught up in someone else's mouth: resonance. A woman hums along with my hairdryer, taking breaths when she needs to, stopping starting glottal on the same note, and then shrill glissando and more gurgle laughing. He turns the dryer to low and she moans approval, relief. The laugh track carries on and sounds silly now against the serious real life, "Ouch. My chin."

I turn on the reading light by the bed and it tightens up the room. I take my suit jacket off, the silk blouse, and I'm glad I wore this bra; I always do on the road. Sixty dollars in the mail from the back of a magazine about smart working women. "What's that supposed to look like?" Richard, date three. I like to know I have it on when I'm talking to men like the owner of this hotel. This morning, I sat back in his chair, my nipples crept out through lace to touch silk and I knew a sexual moment had wandered between us. All common sense. I knew I would never have to take that fat man to court; he would never hold me responsible for something somebody else did wrong.

My hair is a mess. I still wear the skirt, but the pantyhose and white cotton are gone gone gone. I packed high heels; they lift. The knock is quiet this time; I give it a moment to sink in and then take my glass to the door knowing my lips are stained. I am tall and straight, my nipples emerge past where my blouse should be.

"Oh. Yikes. Sorry," she says to me. "Thanks," and hands me the hairdryer, cord wrapped tightly around the barrel. Dressed up in a policeman's uniform and black stilettos, she is on her way to work. Her hair is white blonde and enormous under the patent leather cap. The tie is a nice authentic touch except for the pink sequins. Night stick hanging down in front on a piece of leather; her breasts are much . . .

"Never never never marry someone just because you like his mother. It's okay to like the mother, just don't marry him because of her. Too many complications. He wants you to be her, you want to be her, she likes you because you're not like him, you like her because she's a little like him. You think she is how he'll turn out, but he's always the boy, you're always the mom. And there are things you can only do to your mom: yell at her like your father always did, leave the dishes for her, not buy toilet paper, whine. And some things you can never do to your mom: lick, toe fuck."

"He doesn't sound like such a bad guy." The owner of this hotel is behind the bar, taking his turn and chatting me up to plunder time. This morning I was a stranger. By now he knows too much, but there may be a way I can rescue the possibility of good sex from this conversation. I think I've scared him, but I can fix that.

He is a big man, not as fat as I thought. His face is happier than it was in his office, his eyes less drab. There is a small tattoo on one wrist, a circle with what is supposed to be a face but the eyes ran. I thought copper bracelets were just seventies superstition; he doesn't seem the type. He appears grounded in reality, such as it is in this beer parlour; it is dressed up like a cave, the ceiling all black and rocky, imitation flint sparkles on the walls. The policeman has finished her act for the night, she lingers at various tables, and now there is a small country band doing its best to sound big and important. Some people dance but you can tell the music makes it hard to. Only the veterans try it and two-step to every song, "Tennessee Waltz" no exception. *Now I know just how much I have lost.* One woman wears a man's jacket, and her pants are too big, too purple for this cave. *Well I lost my little darlin' the night they were playin'.* The girl has a pretty voice but she never smiles.

"Nice voice," I say to the owner.

"They suck. They're local."

"You mean out-of-towners don't?" I pause and get up the nerve. "Suck I mean."

"I'm done around two. We'll sort it out."

It is four a.m. and I knock the phone down to the floor to make it stop. The owner of this hotel said he'd look after the room; no charge, he said. "Keep the shoes, lose the bra," he said. My crotch is swollen and torn, it burns like every time. I wonder about cystitis because of all the beer and the way we did it. He didn't want to see my face. "This is your better side, sweetheart, trust me." He rammed me for emphasis. Like coupling trains.

"I waited," says Richard. "Should I call back?"
"No. I'm here."
He wants to know if I'm all right. I start from the flight this morning and strive for accuracy. This is not intended to cause him pain and it doesn't any more. He won't write anything down or read the paper while I'm talking. "Two strippers in one day?" I know he is sitting at the kitchen table, dipping a graham cracker into a glass of wine, in the dark. He listens to me. When I tell him about the cowboy dream, he laughs about the couch. "You dream in plaid?" Sometimes I imagine he is looking out the window during the hard-core parts, but I forgive that. Our street is quiet, soft with ornamental fruit trees; cats scratch out nasturtiums in dry dirt below the window, behind the laurel hedge; occasional long distance caterwaul, but not tonight this morning. He pours more wine, I go on at length.

At the end of it, he wants to know: did I dance, do I have sulfa, do I think the stripper on the plane will always wake up sad.

"And now you," I say. "Are *you* all right?"
"Describe the curtains in your room," he says.

Acknowledgements

Sincere thanks to the Canada Council Explorations Program for providing funds which allowed me to work on some of these stories, and to Mark Anthony Jarman, Smaro Kamboureli and even Tom Henry.

Some of these stories appeared first in the following periodicals and anthologies:

"Science Diet," *Prism International* 28.2 (1990).
"Dressing for Hope" (titled "Blessed Candles Headed Somewhere in Flight"), *Canadian Forum* (September 1991).
"Counting Ties," *Canadian Fiction Magazine* 73 (1991).
"Enough Force to Cause Serious Injury," *The Fiddlehead* 167 (1991).
"Play Dominoes," *An Ounce of Cure: Alcohol in the Canadian Short Story*, edited by Mark Anthony Jarman (Victoria: Beach Holme, 1992).
"Round River," *The Malahat Review* (Spring 1994).
"Grief Work," *Canadian Fiction Magazine* (Summer 1994).